T0029703

MIDNIGHT
ON BEACON
STREET

HARPER PERENNIAL

NEW YORK • LONDON • TORONTO • SYDNEY • NEW DELHI • AUCKLAND

MIDNIGHT ON BEACON STREET

A NOVEL

EMILY RUTH VERONA

HARPER ● PERENNIAL

This is a work of fiction. Names, characters, places, and incidents are products of the author's imagination or are used fictitiously and are not to be construed as real. Any resemblance to actual events, locales, organizations, or persons, living or dead, is entirely coincidental.

MIDNIGHT ON BEACON STREET. Copyright © 2024 by Emily Ruth Verona. All rights reserved. Printed in the United States of America. No part of this book may be used or reproduced in any manner whatsoever without written permission except in the case of brief quotations embodied in critical articles and reviews. For information, address HarperCollins Publishers, 195 Broadway, New York, NY 10007.

HarperCollins books may be purchased for educational, business, or sales promotional use. For information, please email the Special Markets Department at SPsales@harpercollins.com.

FIRST EDITION

Designed by Jen Overstreet
Title page photograph © Stephanie Cabrera/Shutterstock

_____

Library of Congress Cataloging-in-Publication Data

Names: Verona, Emily Ruth, author.
Title: Midnight on Beacon Street : a novel / Emily Ruth Verona.
Description: First edition. | New York : Harper Perennial, 2024. |
Identifiers: LCCN 2023038967 (print) | LCCN 2023038968 (ebook) | ISBN 9780063330511 (trade paperback) | ISBN 9780063330528 (ebook)
Subjects: LCGFT: Horror fiction. | Thrillers (Fiction) | Novels.
Classification: LCC PS3622.E754 M53 2024 (print) | LCC PS3622.E754 (ebook) | DDC 813/.6--dc23/eng/20230919
LC record available at https://lccn.loc.gov/2023038967
LC ebook record available at https://lccn.loc.gov/2023038968

_____

ISBN 978-0-06-333051-1

24 25 26 27 28 LBC 6 5 4 3 2

for you, Mom—
love you lots and acres

More than 2,800,000 break-ins were reported in the
United States in 1993.

MIDNIGHT ON BEACON STREET

CHAPTER ONE

BEN

SATURDAY, OCTOBER 16, 1993
12:06 A.M. (6 MINUTES AFTER MIDNIGHT)

The blood beneath Ben's bare feet is too fresh to be sticky. It's hard not to slip. And so, the little boy holds still—so very still. Stiller than he has ever held before. Or will ever hold again. So still that when one of his fingers twitches involuntarily it is as if his whole arm has swung like a pendulum too heavy for his body. It feels like it will twist. Snap. Break off altogether. Fall onto the floor and writhe around in the blood like a beetle on its back. Helpless and alone and desperate to be reattached—to turn back the clock. Undo what has been done.

But it's only a twitch. Or maybe a tremble. And the arm does not fall onto the floor. Into the blood. It does not flop around. It does not squirm like some broken little thing. No, it hangs painfully at his side. Perfectly intact. And nothing changes—not one thing. The room remains quiet, and he remains quiet within it.

It's more than just the blood—the fear of falling in it. The familiarity of the kitchen has scampered off. He no longer recognizes his surroundings. The soft, golden glow from the hallway has stretched out dimly across the kitchen, poisoning the darkness with shadows. It doesn't make sense. The light should make him feel safer, not more scared. Maybe his big sister is right. Maybe everything is better in the dark. When it's dark you can't see your hand in front of your face. You can't see monsters lurking. Ghosts haunting. You can't see what's dead and what's not.

This kitchen—this kitchen, which no longer resembles *his* kitchen—is teeming with wrongness. The possibility of more wrongness. Monsters. Ghosts. The dead—

There is something dead here.

Someone dead here.

Did the ghost do it? No. Amy said it's a nice ghost. *Maybe* it's a nice ghost. He wants to ask its name so it will go away, but he can't speak. His heart is drumming in his ears. Like a guitar string strumming. The consistency of it is making him dizzy—his head swirling and swirling. Ice cream twisting out of the spout and into a cone. His heart is pounding and his ears are hot and his hands are going numb at the fingertips. His eyes, wide as twin moons, are dry. He can't blink. If he blinks, she might move, and he will have missed it.

Only—

Her face—

It's not going to move.

Not unless this is a dream.

Could it be? No. Dreams don't leave a wetness under your feet.

And dreams don't—they *can't* do this.

His wide, dry, swirling eyes pore across the face in front of him—those hard edges and gentle curves. The softness of her skin, because it still looks soft. Even now. The realness of it all seems big and bulky and almost cartoonish—like his brain can't quite process what he's seeing, and so it's begun to take everything apart, reconstructing the scene in a way that is easier to digest, making everything appear plastic and waxy. Fake. Her eyes are half open, like a doll's. M hates dolls. Says they look dead. She's right. They do. Little glass marbles for eyes. Colorful and smiling, but dead—dead—dead—*dead*.

Bile rushes up his throat, full and thick and burning.

It rises with the intake of each breath, and falls back down again with every exhale.

He almost pukes, but doesn't.

Almost screams, but can't.

The Fear is coursing through his veins, pulsing through them. Pure and thick and hard. Making his insides heavy. Solid. Turning him to stone. That's it, surely, he's becoming stone. Just like in the story M told him about the woman who looked back when she shouldn't have and turned to stone.

No—that wasn't stone. That was salt. She turned to salt.

Maybe he is turning to salt.

Still petrified, Ben's eyes roll in his skull—lowering until he can just barely make out the edge of the blade. It's shiny. And red. So red. The color is practically burning a hole through time and space. His fingers tighten around the handle of the knife—his little fingers all lined together—and he swallows hard. Only his mouth is too dry, causing that swallow to feel like a groan. Or a choke. He is choking. And the bile is coming and he can't breathe.

He doesn't want to look back at the dead girl's face, but he forces himself to do it. Or rather, his eyes force themselves to do it, without the consent of his brain. He doesn't know why. He's begging them to stop. His eyes are determined though—more than determined. Dry and wide and desperate to see—

Slippery blood and marble eyes and skin like wax.

Her body is slumped against the base of the counter, one palm facing up and open, the other limp against the floor. Blood spreads across the linoleum and fills in the creases around that big gold-and-silver ring on her index finger. He shifts his weight suddenly and—without meaning to—his toes slide against the slickness of the blood.

Red beneath him. Around him. Everywhere. His brain pulsing. He still can't feel his hands—not since that twitch that might as well have been a bone snapping. A deep breath escapes through his nose, but he can't seem to draw one back in. This is it. This is how he's going to die. Because he still can't breathe—won't breathe. Can your body do that? Take all the air away? Kill you? Can your body murder itself like that? His body's doing it. Right now. Turning him to salt. Because he's seeing something he shouldn't be seeing.

His teeth, having been clenched all the while, keep that unsung scream locked somewhere low in his chest. It bangs against his ribs, trying to break free. But it doesn't.

His body won't let it. Because his body is trying to kill him.

Salt, salt, salt.

Vision blurry, his eyes slowly focus on her face, because even with all this blood and all this stillness, he is waiting. Watching. Expecting everything to change. Convincing himself that it just might.

And maybe, if he waits long enough, the dead will come back to life.

If he's patient.

If his body doesn't kill him.

If the ghost doesn't get him.

If he doesn't turn to salt first.

CHAPTER TWO

AMY

FRIDAY, OCTOBER 15, 1993
5:15 P.M. (6 HOURS AND 45 MINUTES BEFORE MIDNIGHT)

Amy walks into the kitchen and sees Eleanor Mazinski fixing herself a cocktail she won't have time to finish. She does this before every date; she says it's to calm her nerves. Not that Amy would describe Eleanor as a naturally nervous person. She's the opposite. Bold. Fearless. Fun. The type of mother everyone wants and no one ever gets—the jackpot of moms. Linda Hamilton in *Judgment Day*, as opposed to Linda Hamilton in *The Terminator*. Not that Eleanor could be directly compared to Sarah Connor exactly. She's nothing like her in fact, but Amy can recognize that Eleanor is a cool mom and Chase Hills is a small, quiet town desperately lacking in cool moms. Pretty typical for New Jersey suburbia, as far as Amy can tell.

Eleanor's coolness can probably be attributed to the fact that she is much younger than the other moms Amy knows. She's only twenty-eight. More like a big sister than a mom. Amy loves her own mother—she does—but she knows that hers is your typical *mom* mom. The normal kind. Her mother and Eleanor have very little in common, except perhaps for the way they love. Both women love their kids. Amy can see that plainly.

Still, there's something otherworldly about Eleanor Mazinski and her red hair and green eyes and perfect cheekbones. The way she dances around the counter, popping two cherries into her martini and sipping carefully so as not to disturb her lipstick. Her dress looks about ten years old, but it works, the bright green fabric flattering at all the right curves—curves as flawless as that swirling red hair and those emerald eyes and her marble-carved cheeks. There's a certain liveliness about the dress that suits her, accentuating her inner Eleanor-ness.

"Amy!" The smile painted so decadently across her face is broad and fresh and vibrant.

She's practically giddy at the sight of the seventeen-year-old, who waves back without a word.

In Eleanor's presence Amy feels like a moldy, lumpy pear. And plain too—her dark brown hair dull and shapeless. She pulls her backpack up on her shoulder, adjusting the strap. Her black T-shirt is a little overwashed and starting to look gray, though it's mostly covered by her grandfather's old, oversize navy-blue jacket with the large lapels. The one he used to wear in the forties or fifties. "Loving this," Eleanor declares, taking note of the teenager's black tights and burgundy plaid skirt. Amy knows her thighs are thick—her waistline too— and was nervous about the skirt, but Eleanor's praise fortifies her. At least someone understands. Amy's become a mystery to all her friends. They can't figure out when exactly she stopped buying polos and started dressing like a "Soundgarden groupie," which was the exact phrasing Whitney used. She doubts Whitney—who aspires to marry a future senator and move to Connecticut—even knows what a Soundgarden groupie looks like. But Amy does know and Whitney isn't wrong.

That's the thing about girls you've known since preschool—they act surprised when you're no longer a chipper little copy of your former self. They say Amy is turning on them. Joining the counterculture. Really, she's just trying to fade out—disappear. That's why she's been wearing her grandfather's coat everywhere. To hide who she is underneath. She uses it as decoy skin. So that she won't have to explain herself. Defend herself. She's not entirely sure what kind of person she wants to be yet, so why should she give everyone the opportunity to go ahead and make assumptions?

"Hi," Amy replies at last, because she has to say something and Ms. Mazinski doesn't like to be called Ms. Mazinski. Amy isn't quite comfortable saying "Eleanor" out loud though. To circumvent this trap, she avoids names and titles entirely, which is something she's been doing with her friends' parents for years. The older she gets the harder it is to pinpoint where exactly she stands: no longer a child but not quite grown. Saying "Mr." and "Mrs." makes her feel infantile, but first names—first names suggest equality, intimacy.

"I used the key you gave me," she continues. "I hope you don't mind . . ."

"Not at all, not at *all*." Eleanor takes another sip before leaving the martini on the counter. The yellow laminate complements the linoleum flooring, which is designed in such a way as to give the appearance of tiles. Each "tile" is patterned in brown and harvest yellow with little floral accents. All the appliances are yellow, too, albeit in a paler shade. The fridge. The stove. It's like the kitchen you'd see in a 1970s sitcom or the house Amy's grandparents used to live in. This whole setup isn't Eleanor's style, that's for sure. But she bought the place as it was, most of the furniture included, and hasn't made any changes. She says she's too busy to bother, but Amy's pretty sure she would have redecorated already if she could afford to do it. Eleanor does not strike her as the sort of person to let the past creep up on her like this.

Fortunately, the house was in pretty good condition when Eleanor bought it, functional at least if not exactly stylish. The contrast between the house and Eleanor herself is completely striking, causing the latter to look even more glamorous and fashionable in comparison. A pearl in its oyster shell.

With a smile, Eleanor comes and takes Amy's hands in her own. "You are my angel, you know that, right? I don't know what I'd do without you."

Eleanor's hands are warm and soft, perfumed from some sort of lotion that smells like airy lavender. Amy has been babysitting around the neighborhood for two years now, since she was fifteen. Eleanor Mazinski is the first one of her customers to ever give her a key. Or call her an angel. Or make Amy sad that they aren't somehow friends. She flashes a self-conscious smile. "Where are your other angels?"

The laugh that escapes Eleanor is shrewd but warm. "More like devils tonight. They've been arguing nonstop since I got home. I think M got into a fight at school, but she won't say a word about it. Stubborn creature. God forbid that girl ever decides to go on a hunger strike—Oh! Before I forget, B's got that book fair brochure thing." Eleanor points to it on the kitchen table in the corner. "He'll want to fill out the order form in the back, and he can, but don't let him put it in his backpack. We're going to see which ones the library has first . . . if we even have time this weekend. There's so much I haven't done yet. I swear, Friday nights are just murder. Why do men always want to go out on Friday nights? Are they that lonely? Have they not heard of Saturday?"

Amy shrugs. With all the babysitting, she and her boyfriend usually have to settle for Sunday dates. No one ever needs a sitter on Sunday night. There's still school the next day, so she and Miles can't stay out too late, but they make do. "Who are you seeing?" Amy asks, a little shy, because she knows Eleanor is older and wiser and generally more interesting than herself. She arches her shoulders back, tilting her head. Trying to play the part of the girlfriend. The confidante. And Eleanor lets her. Maybe Eleanor wishes they were friends too.

"Pedro in HR set me up with his wife's cousin." Eleanor sighs, scrunching her face and returning to her martini. She takes a long sip, her lipstick leaving a skeletal red print on the glass, and shakes her head. "To be honest, I don't exactly have high hopes. He's an accountant, and accountants, as you know, are notoriously disappointing dancers."

Amy does not in fact know, but she nods like she does. Eleanor doesn't talk to her like she's a teenager. She talks to her like they've known each other forever. Like they're equals. Amy really likes this, especially in comparison to some of the other parents she sits for. There are also no leering dads at Eleanor's either. Amy caught a dad doing that one time—at a house she doesn't sit for anymore—and ever since then she's found herself wondering if some of them are eying her even when she knows they're not. Last month, Mr. Taylor asked what colleges she'd applied to, and Amy, convinced he was trying to look down her shirt, hastily buttoned her jacket and fumbled trying to remember the name of a school. Any school. Only she couldn't. Rutgers had gone and popped out of her head. Sarah Lawrence too. Even UCLA—not that she would have mentioned it. Her parents don't know she's applied or that she wants to study film, become a cinematographer in the vein of Daniel Pearl or Nicholas Musuraca. Or maybe even a producer like Debra Hill. They could probably get on board with the filmmaking part, but she doubts they'd be okay with her packing up and moving to the other side of the country. She isn't even sure *she'd* be comfortable with it. If she gets in. She probably won't get in. Why did she even apply?

After three or four minutes of painfully awkward silence with Mr. Taylor, Amy mumbled something about not having decided yet and darted out the door so fast she might as well have been on fire. Her and her no-good brain—feeding its own damn fear of being afraid. As a kid, her parents brought her to a specialist. When that specialist diagnosed her with generalized anxiety and panic disorder, her father decided that Amy should stop seeing her. As if running from the diagnosis would somehow undo the very existence of it.

Did it work? Of course not.

And through the years, the panic attacks have only been getting worse.

Ever since the disaster with Mr. Taylor—who was probably just trying to be nice, but who can even know for certain?—Amy has taken to wearing baggy sweatshirts to all the houses now. No makeup. Except for when she goes to Eleanor's. This morning, Whitney laughed and said that the Mazinski house is Amy's hottest date spot.

"Same as last time," Eleanor continues, pouring out the rest of her drink and placing the empty glass next to the sink. "In bed by nine. They don't have to be asleep, but at least in their rooms. The microwave has decided to stop microwaving so I do not recommend trying it—the kids haven't eaten yet so I ordered you all a pizza. Money is by the front door. Is Miles coming by later?"

Amy hesitates, then nods. None of the other parents ever let her boyfriend stay—just drop her off or pick her up when her mom takes the car and she needs a ride. Eleanor doesn't just not mind him being here. She encourages it. For someone who hasn't had the best luck with relationships, she's relatively smitten with the idea of Amy and Miles and their young love. *He's absolutely adorable*, Eleanor had said that first night when he dropped her off at the house. *A dark-haired River Phoenix! And he looks at you like you're a Greek goddess!*

"Making out is fine after the kids are in bed, but please, no sex," Eleanor stipulates. "I had to learn the hard way that my little insomniac hears *everything*. I don't want M walking in on you two doing anything . . . *compromising*."

"Oh, no—we wouldn't," Amy stammers, her cheeks red. *Wouldn't* really means *haven't*, but she doesn't say this. Because she likes the idea that Eleanor sees her as someone who would have sex. Might have it in a stranger's home even. Isn't completely terrified at the thought of the logistics involved in being naked for the very first time with a boy.

"I know, I know—you're perfect," Eleanor sighs dreamily. "I don't deserve you."

Amy pivots from the praise. "Where are you meeting him tonight?"

Eleanor smirks, for in the short time they've known one another she has learned rather quickly how awkward the teenager can get. How she asks questions to shield herself. *Shy is fine*, Eleanor had said that first night. *Just don't be meek. There's a huge difference. And people can smell it on you.*

Can Eleanor smell it on her? The insecurity? The propensity for hesitation? She doesn't hide it well, but no one ever calls her out on it. Except for Whitney. Whitney sees everything. Remembers everything. That girl's brain is a complete catalogue of events, dates, and indiscretions.

"That Japanese place near the car dealership in Morris Plains." Eleanor says this as if the idea is a lavish one. "Do you know it?"

Amy shakes her head.

"You should make Miles take you some time. It's fabulous."

Eleanor Mazinski has two rules for dating: don't let them pick you up, and always choose the restaurant yourself. That way, if the date is no good, at least you'll like the food. And strange men won't know where you live. "I will," Amy assures her.

Last time, Eleanor recommended an Italian restaurant in Parsippany. She and Miles went the following Sunday—they didn't have school on Monday because of a Jewish holiday—and it was very romantic. Not too expensive. He got the chicken marsala and she ordered a steak with sautéed onions. Miles teased her after dinner for having onion breath, and the second he got up to go to the bathroom Amy popped not one or two but four pieces of gum in her mouth.

Did she bring gum tonight? The pack in her backpack was empty yesterday and she can't remember if she grabbed a new one . . .

"All the windows are locked," Eleanor adds. "I know it's freezing out and there's no reason to open one, but just thought you should know. With these burglaries happening I'd rather be safe than sorry."

Amy nods. Her parents have been the same way the last few weeks. Usually, Chase Hills is the kind of place where you probably don't even need to lock your door, but the recent spate of break-ins across the county have everyone on edge. "Windows will stay locked," Amy assures her. "Doors too."

"Excellent!" chirps Eleanor, crossing the kitchen into the hallway. She grips the side of the oak banister with perfectly polished nails—long, crimson, and glossy—and hollers up the stairs. "M! B! A is here!"

Dropping her backpack on the floor between the hallway and the living room, Amy listens as the silence upstairs gives way to the clamor of feet. The six-year-old boy is the first one down, the most eager to please. Soft, fair, somewhat uneven brown hair and big round eyes. A long cord around his neck with something called a mezuzah dangling around his navel. According to Eleanor, a mezuzah is placed in the doorway of a Jewish house, but, after all the moving they've done, Ben feels safest having a miniature one on himself too.

Ben stops at the foot of the stairs, his lips crooking as if they might give way to a smile if not for his own inherent timidity. Eleanor claims that he gets this trait from her mother—Ben's grandmother. She says it fondly, but Amy gets the impression that Eleanor and her mother are not close. Haven't been for a long time. There are pictures of Eleanor's own grandmother, Nana as they all call her, in the living room, but not a single photo of Eleanor's parents.

Ben fidgets a little nervously. Amy grins and waves, which sends a little ripple of pinkness across his cheeks as his sister comes up beside him. She is twelve and far ahead of her brother in terms of sass and disinterest. Her wavy hair—redder than her mother's—has recently been cut, and professionally too, Amy figures, based on the way it's resting very finely just above her shoulders. There's a sparkly purple scrunchie on her wrist, and her green sweatshirt, likely stolen from her mother's closet, hangs loose on one of her shoulders. Her bare feet expose a collection of freshly painted toenails. The same shade of red as her mother's fingers. Bolder and darker than their hair. She stops on the last step and rests her arms on the banister. Disappointed. Last time Mira told Amy that she was too old for a babysitter. This was about an hour before she spent thirty minutes looking for a stuffed dog she refused to go to sleep without. Most sitters would consider her a preteen nightmare, but Amy thinks there's something to be admired in Mira's resolve. She even envies it just a little bit—the way Mira retains her own self. Amy was never so outspoken—so defiant—at that age.

She's not even that outspoken now.

"So," begins Eleanor, placing a hand on her hip and immediately garnering her children's rapt attention. "Amy is in charge. I want you to accept her word as the word of God, understand? She tells you to do something and you listen."

A pout from Mira. "What if she tells us to jump off a bridge?"

Eleanor's narrowed eyes glint. A grin slips seamlessly across her face. "Then, my love," she says, tapping her daughter under the chin tenderly, "you close your eyes and jump."

Mira rolls her eyes, while Ben continues to stare at Amy—nearly, but still not quite, on the verge of smiling. Trying to gather up the courage to do it maybe. Or else just trying to hide the fact that he wants so very much to smile at her. The babysitter sees much of her own reserve in him, more so than in any of the other kids she watches. She's only been over here a few times, but already she feels inherently protective of him, as if he were her own little brother.

"Pizza should be here soon," Eleanor continues. "Are you hungry?"

Mira nods. Ben shakes his head.

"The number for the restaurant is on the fridge," Eleanor tells them. "But Amy is the only one allowed to use it. Phone is off limits. My *makeup* is off limits," she adds, eyeing Mira keenly with that last note. "Got it?"

Collectively they nod—Mira a little unwillingly, as she fusses with her scrunchie and licks her lips. Ben continues to stare adamantly at Amy. The edge of his mouth curves upward in a half smile.

"Please be good," Eleanor begs of them. "Really. Just try, all right? Who knows? You might enjoy it."

Mira snorts. *"Yeah, right."*

The line of Eleanor's jaw stiffens. "There is ice cream in it for you tomorrow if you're good."

Mira shrugs. "I'd prefer cash."

"Wouldn't we all, my love."

"They'll be great," Amy assures everyone hastily. As far as kids go, these two aren't very much trouble at all. Not compared to the hyperactive Dumont twins she watches on Landon Street and the Miller's screeching two-year-old on Allen Avenue. Amy fiddles with the big, clunky two-tone gold-and-silver ring on her index finger, a comforting lump of hammered metal. It can't keep her from fidgeting. She's certain adulthood isn't prepared to agree with her—doesn't agree with her now. Sometimes she finds herself jealous of the kids she watches. They are so young. She wasn't having full-on panic attacks yet when she was their age . . . and when was her last one now? Only a week ago?

No—yesterday. She was driving to the mall to pick up Halloween decorations, fake spider webs for the bushes out front, and she missed the exit. She didn't know how to turn around at the next one—she'd never driven down that way before. The worst part—the very worst part—was that this was precisely what she'd always feared. Taking a wrong turn. Getting lost. It was a worry that swelled in her every time she drove. After she missed the exit for the mall, she'd had to pull over to the side of the road because she couldn't breathe and her hands were shaking too violently to keep the steering wheel straight.

Amy finds herself spiraling back into the memory and tries to pull herself out of it—out of the haze and into the *here*. The *now*. She watches as Eleanor pretends to glare sternly at Mira. Mira pretends to hate it. Then, with a gentler look, Eleanor gives each child a kiss on the cheek. "All right!" she sings. "I'm off!"

Her son's ardent, serious eyes blossom quickly to life. He just about stumbles down the stairs, hurrying to Eleanor before she can reach the door. "Will you be back before we go to bed?"

"*Seriously?*" Mira tosses her head back with a groan.

Ben gazes from his mother to Mira to his mother again. Waiting. Hoping. Eleanor plants another kiss on the top of Ben's head. Strokes his cheek. "I will try, B. Okay?"

He nods reluctantly, and she runs her fingers through his hair. When she reaches the doorway she stops, kissing her fingers before pressing them against the metal mezuzah in the doorway. Amy has seen her do this every time she's left the house. She doesn't know what it means.

"Have a good time," says Amy.

Eleanor stops halfway out the door, tilts her head back, and laughs. "A woman in this world should be so lucky!"

Having bitten so hard on the inside of her cheek that she could taste blood, Amy avoided looking into the mirror by pretending to notice a toothpaste stain on the countertop. Her mother finished applying a stroke of subdued dark-blue eye shadow and leaned back to study the full effect. "Do you want me to teach you how to do this sometime?" she asked, knowing eleven-year-old Amy was paying attention even if she was pretending to look bored.

Amy shook her head, the inside of her mouth watery and metallic.

Her mother gave a soft smile. "It's not hard. I promise."

There was no way Amy believed this to be true, but she knew better than to say so. Her mother would only try to help her, coax her out of her comfort zone. The less confidence Amy showed the more her mother tried to build her up, raise her spirits. Little did she know that the more encouragement she gave her daughter, the more that overcompensation bit into Amy's skin, making her feel more hopeless than before. "Do you have to go?" asked Amy, near pouting but not quite. She was too old for that.

Her mother sighed. "It's your Uncle Andrew's birthday. Just be glad you don't have to go." The party was at some fancy restaurant Amy couldn't remember the name of. Adults only. With an open bar. Her mother looked at her. "If I could get away with staying home in my pj's, I would."

Amy leaned back against the pale-blue poppy-field wallpaper across from the bathtub. "Can't Charlie and Donnie come over at least?"

"After that movie they let you watch?" she was suppressing a laugh. "You're lucky your father didn't skin them."

Amy sulked. She missed her old babysitter, the one who'd gone off to college. Nancy. The sitter they'd tried after Nancy left hadn't worked out, and Amy was leery of whoever her mother had managed to come up with this time. Sensing this reluctance, Amy's mother tried to give a sympathetic smile. "The new girl is lovely, you'll like her. And she can help tutor you in math."

Staring hard at her toes, Amy knew she'd much prefer her delinquent cousins and their scary movies to some math tutor.

Her mother leaned in and put her hands on her knees, tempting Amy to peer up at her from lowered lids. "Try her out for tonight, okay? If you don't hit it off, we can look for someone else. Deal?"

Amy wanted to argue, but she also didn't want to get in the way, so she nodded without a word. Her mother planted a kiss on her cheek before taking a tube of lipstick off the counter and removing the top. It was a vivid red her mother hardly ever wore. The doorbell let out a shrill little chime then. Her mother's eyes darted from the mirror as she blotted her lipstick.

Amy frowned. "She's early."

"Nancy was always early and you adored her for it—now, go get the door, will you?"

She would have protested if her mother was still paying attention but she wasn't, so Amy quietly left the bathroom and walked down the narrow hallway into the living room. Her father must not have come back yet—he'd gone out to get gas—otherwise he would have made it from his recliner to the door before her. Indulgently, Amy took her time. The doorbell rang again, and if she stalled for too long her mother would come out to scold her, so Amy checked the window and twisted the door handle.

The door swung open and a bright-eyed, fresh-faced fifteen-year-old girl was waiting with an armful of books and a dimpled smile on her face. She had short blond hair with thick bangs. The blue sweater she wore only highlighted her glimmering teal eyes. "Hi there, peanut!" the teenager beamed. "You must be Amy."

CHAPTER FOUR

BEN

FRIDAY, OCTOBER 15, 1993
11:55 P.M. (5 MINUTES BEFORE MIDNIGHT)

Draping his comforter over the side of the bed, Ben hops onto the plush, dark-blue carpet and goes to the window. He pulls on the cord and the blinds go up halfway, leaning at an awkward slant because they've been broken ever since they moved in, and Mom hasn't tried to fix them. She hasn't tried to fix anything. The loose handles on his dresser—M is the one who tightened them. Made sure they wouldn't pop off every time he went to find a shirt. He should ask her how she did it, so he knows for next time. If he knows how to do it, then he could teach Mom how to do it too. M wouldn't tell him, though, not even if he got up the nerve to ask. She likes keeping her secrets. Always has.

There are no streetlamps on Beacon Street—which M thinks is funny for some reason—and the moon tonight is too small to cast any light on the rooftops or trees or the fire hydrant at the end of their driveway. Fire hydrants are supposed to be red, but this one is yellow. Mom says it's because it doesn't work. Broken fire hydrants are painted yellow. This worries Ben, but only a little. What if there's a fire? How will they put it out?

Even though there's plenty of darkness blanketing the neighborhood, Mr. Darren's study across the street is still lit, glowing like the block's very own nightlight. Mr. Darren teaches at a college and is something called an *insomac*, so he's always awake. At least that's what M says. Ben doesn't know if it's true. Sometimes M likes to make things up, just to see if she can get away with it. Usually she can, and it bothers him. But only a little. Because he doesn't know how to make things up. At least, he wouldn't know how to get anyone to believe him if he did, so he might as well not even try. *Insomac* is a real word, though—he's heard Mom say it before. About M. He tried to ask his teacher at school what it means, but after she had him repeat it a few times she only stared at him with a completely puzzled look. Like she had no idea what he was talking about. He's not sure if she was actually confused or if she was just surprised. Mrs. Marker likes math and barely spends any time on their study words. And their study words are mostly one or two syllables. *Insomac*, that's—three? Four? He claps it out.

IN-SO-MAC.

Three, then. And that's a lot.

He's not surprised that M knows it, though. M knows lots of big words. Bad words, too, but she rarely uses those. Mom wouldn't like it. She gets these words from books—all kinds of books. The American Girl series used to be her favorite. She liked Felicity because she had red hair and knew how to ride horses and was really brave. She reads other books now, though—thicker books with lots of big words and fancy meanings. She took *Tom Sawyer* out of the library last week. Read it in three days. Ben is always trying to get her to read to him, but M says that he's old enough now and needs to be able to do it himself.

He can read—he tries—but he still has trouble with it. He knows M was already reading chapter books at his age. She's always been a good reader, but it's harder for him than it was for her. Sometimes he gets the letters all mixed up. Sometimes he thinks a letter is supposed to make one sound, but then it goes and makes a different one instead. Then there's the shape of the letters themselves. He confuses his lowercase q's and his lowercase *p*'s, his lowercase *d*'s and his lowercase *b*'s. Why can't everything just be written in capital letters? They're so much easier—nice and clear and big.

Mom says it doesn't matter that he's not all too good at reading. She says he's good at other things. She never actually says what those things are, but she insists he's good at them.

Staring out at Mr. Darren's bright little window, Ben studies the way the light stretches out across his bushes and over the front walk. Something small and gray darts through the shadows into Mr. Darren's bushes—a cat, probably. Cats aren't very noisy.

The wind, on the other hand—the wind has been howling lately. Mom likes to pretend it's a pack of wolves trying to whistle. She thinks that's pretty funny. Ben doesn't think Chase Hills has wolves, but he's been too afraid to ask. M would love it if there were wolves—they're just like dogs, she says. Only bigger. Scarier. Exactly the sort of animal she'd want to be if she could be an animal. There probably aren't any wolves. Chase Hills isn't the kind of place that has big, dangerous creatures—the ones with teeth the size of fingers.

M says the town is like this because it is boring. Mom says Chase Hills is quiet because it's safe. All Ben knows is that Mom still stays out too late and M still goes to the bathroom three hundred thousand times a night. That's what woke him in the first place. At first, he thought maybe it was the ghost or the Cat Man—because the Cat Man likes to creep into houses—but then he realized it had to be M. The bathroom is right next to his room, and Mom tells M not to flush the toilet at night because it's loud, but she never listens and so it sends the pipes screaming through his bedroom wall.

The toilet at their old apartment in Pinton was just as noisy—noisier, probably, because everything about Pinton was noisier—but it blended in with all the other sounds. Trains coming in and out of the station down the street and people stumbling around yelling in the dark. Sometimes they laughed. Sometimes they argued. But whatever they did, they made sure to shout while they were doing it. That's the difference between cities and small towns, M says. City people shout at your face. Small town people whisper behind your back.

When the pipes grumble here, the sound of it sticks out against the starkness of the quiet. Like an animal dying. Or a baby shrieking. Running his finger across the windowsill, Ben presses his face close to the glass—trying to get a look at the driveway below. Mom forgot to leave the light on out there and so everything is shadowed in that vague way picture book backgrounds are shaded in. The glass is cool and smooth against his skin. When a breath escapes from between his lips it fogs the window.

Mom might already be down there. She could be sitting in the driveway, fussing with her keys. Or fixing her lipstick. Or filing a hangnail. Or trying to convince the tape deck to work. She says you have to be nice to it, say *please* and *thank you* or else it will chew up the cassettes.

Mom takes longer to get out of the car than anyone Ben has ever known, not that he's known a great many people. He didn't really have a lot of friends back in Pinton. Still hasn't really made any in Chase Hills, except for Steve—if he counts. They've been sitting together at lunch and Steve seems determined to turn them into friends. He's nice enough and certainly talks plenty. M tells Ben he should be more sociable, but around Steve it's difficult to get a word in—not that Ben hasn't had plenty of practice listening. M is a major rambler when it comes to books. That's what Mom calls her anyway. And Mom knows, she says, because she's a rambler too.

So why isn't he?

What part was left out when he was put together?

M used to tell him that it's because he's an extraterrestrial, but he didn't know what that meant. He asked M, but she refused to tell him, and when he asked Mom, she laughed and laughed and finally, when she stopped laughing, told him that M was wrong. He wasn't an alien. Then she went on to explain what it meant, and Ben got mad at M for trying to convince him that she wasn't really his sister and that Mom wasn't really his mom. That's how he found out she likes to lie sometimes. And that she's better at it than he would have thought.

She did have a point, though, even if she wasn't telling the truth. He feels smaller than them, not just in age but in being. More bottled up. Mom and M think he's quiet because he's scared all the time, but that's not it—not all of it, at least. Mom likes to pet his head, curl a lock of his hair between her fingers, and tell him he's her favorite listener. That there's no one in the world she'd rather talk to than him. Except if that were true then she'd be home by now.

But she isn't.

And it's getting late.

He could try to ask M about it, but he won't. She usually falls back asleep after she goes to the bathroom, and she wouldn't like him waking her up all over again. He doesn't want to get locked in the closet either. She's always threatening to do that. At their old apartment there was this little coat closet across from the bathroom, and it wasn't very deep or very wide, and there were always ants getting in and crawling around in the space where the floor met the wall. She said if he bothered her, she'd stick him in there and the ants would eat him up, only she never went through with locking him in the closet. Or anywhere. Because she knew it would upset Mom—more than when she says bad words or tells lies. And as mean as M tries to be, she doesn't like to upset Mom.

Leaning his head against the wall, Ben sits on his knees and watches Mr. Darren's window. The shades are drawn so he can't see what's going on inside. Maybe he's an *insomac*, too, like Mr. Darren. Like M. Maybe that's why he hasn't slept through the night in the three months they've lived here.

Ben looks back across his own room. After having stared good and long at Mr. Darren's window, everything around him looks blacker than it had before. He shifts his weight and feels something digging into his leg and runs his fingers across the floor. He pulls the sharp lump of plastic up to the window, examining it carefully.

Oh.

T. R.

Mom's the one who named him. Short for T. rex. Ben hasn't really been playing with his dinosaurs—not since M told him all his plastic figures are for babies—but T. R. is his favorite. The first dinosaur he ever got. Mom tells him this story all the time, about how it was his third birthday and she wanted so much to get him a whole set but they were short on cash at the time and so she picked out this one little fella—because she liked the look of him. And she thought he would protect her B. He doesn't know why M hates his dinosaurs so much. She still has Sammy, her stuffed golden retriever with the green collar, but when Ben tried to say she was too old for Sammy, she punched him in the arm.

Mom doesn't think dinosaurs are for babies. And she insists Mr. Spielberg doesn't either. Over the summer *Jurassic Park* came out and Mom got all excited—it was a chance to show her little boy real dinosaurs. She talked about it for weeks, her face glowing and her eyes bright. M kept reminding her that they weren't *actually* real, but Mom didn't care. She took them to the movies, sent the two of them to the bathroom, and bought herself a ticket. Then, after the attendant had ripped it in half, she waited for him to look away and snuck M and Ben in before anyone noticed. Mom's always sneaking them into movies. Ben thinks it's because the movies she takes them to aren't always for kids, but M says it's because they can't afford to buy so many tickets.

Jurassic Park wasn't like any of the other movies he'd seen before, or the cartoons he'd watched on TV. And the T. rex—it was bigger and realer than he could have imagined. He had nightmares for a month after that, waking up screaming because he thought raptors had broken into their kitchen. It was worth it, though—just to hear that T. rex roar, to watch it move, see it come *alive*.

That night when they got home from the movies, he told Mom he wanted to be a paleontologist. This seemed to please her, which only made him sure it was what he wanted to do. For a few weeks Mom jokingly called him P instead of B. She was surprised when he said he didn't want to be one for Halloween, though. She'd assumed he'd be all for it, but Ben didn't see the point. Costumes are for things you know you'll never be. Monsters. Zombies. Princes. Knights. The idea of dressing up like a paleontologist just for fun makes him feel further away from it. Like it's something he will never actually get to do. You need to go to college to become a paleontologist, and M says there's no way either one of them is ever going. "Why not?" he'd asked one time. She laughed and threw a pretzel at him. "College costs money," she said. "And do *you* think we have money?" Mom wasn't in the kitchen when M told him this or else she would have been mad. She doesn't like it when M talks about money—or, more specifically, how they don't have money. She believes you don't need to be rich to have a good life, which doesn't make any sense because all the best things that have happened for them have been because of money.

Money got them this house, and having a house is something Mom has always wanted for them. Money bought T. R. and all their food and their clothes and the tapes Mom listens to all the time—or some of the tapes, anyway. M insists Mom never paid for anything she got before 1989. Only Mom says stealing is wrong, so this must not be true. It must be one of M's lies.

Ben shifts his weight uncomfortably. Mom should really be back by now. What do you even *do* on a date? It's just dinner, right? And dinnertime was hours ago. But Mom likes dancing, too, and dancing can go late. He knows from the parties Mom used to have in Pinton. He doesn't remember them but M does.

Maybe Mom got into an accident. Maybe that's what happened. Maybe he's here waiting and sulking and her car is all torn up on some road somewhere. M is always worrying about things like that. It makes Ben worry too. He's not sure why. It's not like their dad is dead. No. He's just gone. And no one in their family has ever died in a car accident. So why does M worry all the time? Why is he worried now?

Standing up, Ben goes over to the nightstand and puts T. R. there, in between the clock and a loose Scrabble letter he found under the bed when he was looking for his other sneaker this morning. It's the letter A. Mom and M got him to play Scrabble with them last week, but Ben didn't really like it. The words are all just too hard. Every time he thought he had one M would tell him he wasn't spelling it right.

Ben adjusts T. R. so that he's facing the bed and scratches the back of his neck. Mom couldn't have gotten into an accident. No—he's just thinking that because M puts ideas in his head. She puts them there, and then he can't get rid of them. Like a stain that won't come out no matter how many times you wash it.

M is always staining his head with bad ideas. He would hate her for it except she's his only sister and he doesn't want to hate his only sister. Sometimes he wishes he had a different sister—a nicer one—but he knows he shouldn't wish that. It would make Mom sad if she knew. Mom gets scared too sometimes, even if M can't see it. She gets scared and it's up to them to make sure she feels safe. That's the one thing Ben knows he's good at, keeping Mom safe. Or feeling safe. If only protecting your mom could be a subject at school. He knows he would do well then. Because he's had so much practice. And because he can make Mom laugh even when no one else—not even M—can.

From the bed he sees the faint glow from beyond the blinds fade out. Mr. Darren must finally be going to bed. Good thing. It's so late. Ben wishes he was asleep right now. Sometimes Mom gives them water when they can't sleep. That's usually why M is up peeing half the night.

What was it Amy had said? About milk helping? She said she used to have trouble sleeping when she was his age and her dad always gave her milk.

Maybe he should try it. Amy knows more about these things than he does. It's one of the reasons he feels so safe around her. Amy is the type of person who wants to fix things. Ben's never known someone like that before. She wants to fix things, and so she does. He wants to be like this when he's older. Responsible. Reliable. Someone who has more answers than questions. She isn't scared of the ghost. Not one bit.

Ben gets up, grabbing T. R. off the shelf and pulling the toy close to his chest. Yes. He should get a glass of milk, like Amy says. That will solve everything.

CHAPTER FIVE

AMY

"But why?" asks Mira, cocking her head to the side. Unimpressed. She's covering a set of bruised knuckles with her right hand, possibly a result of that fight Eleanor had mentioned. It seems like Mira doesn't want Amy to notice them, and for now, the babysitter is willing to respect that wish and pretend she doesn't.

Amy plucks and discards a long, loose hair from her T-shirt. Her dad says she sheds like a cat. "Because it's fun!" She responds to Mira's reluctance with excessive cheerfulness. Babysitting is really just pretending to be 85 percent cartoon character. Only, sometimes when she smiles too broadly, she feels less like Mickey Mouse and more like Jack Torrance losing his mind in *The Shining*.

Mira shakes her head, red hair wagging from side to side. Voice flat and certain. "No. No, it's not."

Amy sits back and sighs, glancing around the room for something—anything—that might help her. But no luck. This room is just as dated as the kitchen, with a sea green and blue shag rug and pale blue wallpaper. The couch is green, as are the curtains. The room almost feels like it's underwater. There's an end table in the corner and some shelving against the far wall in a different shade of brown. A few pictures—including the one of Eleanor's grandmother, the kids' Nana—are posed there to make the place feel warm. Inviting. Only the photos just look lonely all by themselves, with no knickknacks or books or toys stacked with them. There's a View-Master tilted atop the television set—it's one of those red little things that looks like binoculars, with the blue button on the side. Amy used to have one, but she doesn't know what happened to it. You stick in small, circular cards with tiny pictures on them and when you look through the lenses the images appear big. Vivid. Real. There are four cards stacked next to the View-Master, but they look old and worn out. Perhaps they'd belonged to Eleanor when she was a child.

"Come on, just try it," Amy urges, offering up the bowl. Mira stares down at the tiny pieces of folded-up paper like one of them is going to jump up and bite her. Amy can't tell if it's the nature of the game that Mira objects to, or the fact that a sitter is the one begging her to play it.

At least the pressure in Amy's chest has subsided—for now. Tension usually flares up when the parents first leave—she worries she'll have a panic attack in front of the kids—but it eases after she gets into the swing of things. Not that it disappears entirely. Panic is like the clingstone pit of a plum nestled in her stomach—her very core. She'd have to gut her own insides to shake it loose. The best she can do is manage it, and she's rather good at managing it. Pretending to manage it. She wonders if this makes her an excellent liar.

Not that lying is helping her. Fake enthusiasm is useless. She won't convert Mira. Amy had a steady string of babysitters from kindergarten, when her mom went back to work, all the way into middle school. Her parents had never trusted her alone. But she never resented any of them the way Mira seems to resent her. On the contrary, they were the big sisters she'd never had. Cool. Pretty. Smart. She wanted to be just like them when she got older, which was probably why she'd decided to start sitting in the first place. She was good with kids. Had a friendly face.

In an attempt to salvage the situation, Amy uses that friendliness now as she turns her attention to Ben. He's been quiet on the couch, his legs folded under him and a dark-navy pillow hugged between his arms. He hasn't said a word since Eleanor left. "You want to play?" she asks him cheerfully. "Don't you?"

The line of the boy's mouth remains stiff, but something akin to eagerness flashes through his eyes. He nods.

Amy shakes up the bowl. "Come on then, Mira. What do you have to lose?"

The girl looks her over carefully with an intent, cautious expression. "My dignity."

Amy tries not to laugh. This is her favorite thing about babysitting—the part that serves as a balm for her anxiety. Kids have a way of fixating on easy problems—problems that might seem big at the time, but are much smaller in the grand scheme of things. It serves as a reminder: a person's feelings can deceive. Distort. Not everything is as big as Amy's body makes it out to be. She has to remember this. "Your dignity will survive. Now, pick one."

Rolling her eyes, Mira shoves her hand into the opaque bowl and plucks out a scrap of paper. Amy's written out dozens of these—saves them to bring along whenever she babysits. She's even divided them into different bags based on age groups, only tonight she'd forgotten to grab the five-to-eight bag, so Ben might need a little help. Even so, it's an easy enough game regardless of age. And she finds most kids enjoy it when she brings something—freshening up the evening with a bit of the outside world.

Only Mira isn't most kids—a fact that the twelve-year-old seems hellbent on hammering home. Mira unfolds the little rectangle of paper, her jaw tight as her eyes scan what's been written. Without a word, and tucking a red lock of hair behind her ear, she crumples up the scrap and shoves it into the pocket of her jeans.

"Movie?" Amy guesses. "Book?"

The girl shakes her head, scratching beneath her scrunchie before stretching out her arms in front of her and cutting them through the air over and over and over.

"Swimmer? Bird?"

Ben chimes in: "Fish."

The sound of his voice is so jarring that, at first, Amy almost doesn't know where the noise originated. When she realizes that Ben is the one who has spoken, that the voice didn't come from the TV or the stereo, he's already gone silent again. Amy looks at him, then back at his sister.

Mira nods. "Yeah."

"Wow, good job," Amy says, flashing Ben a smile. The boy accepts her smile like it's a piece of chocolate, grinning back before he can stop himself. Amy almost giggles, and, quickly, Ben tucks that grin away again.

"See," sighs Mira. "I told you this is ridiculous."

Leaning back in the big armchair by the coffee table, Amy crosses her legs and her arms. Mira falls onto the couch dramatically, as if it is in fact hopeless work taking care of a babysitter. This girl tries so hard to sound like her mother. What's most impressive, perhaps, is how she manages to succeed at it. Knowing all the right ways to tilt her head and shift her eyes; knowing just what to say and how to say it to maximum effect.

Refusing to admit defeat, Amy raises her chin upward. "Well then, Miss Mira, what do you do for fun on a Friday night?"

The girl's brow narrows like she's just stepped in gum and now has to scrape it off her shoe. Amy being the gum, of course. "Read," she declares with a look that says, *Isn't it obvious? Wouldn't you rather be reading?* This is actually the first time Amy's been over when Mira hasn't spent most of the night up in her room.

Amy shrugs. "We can read."

Mira winces. "Together?"

"Not the same book," says Amy. "Just all in the same room."

Before Mira can come up with a proper preteen response or roll her eyes for the fiftieth time, there's a knock at the door. Eyes from both children dart to follow the sound, and Mira's back suddenly goes rigid.

"That must be dinner," Amy declares, popping off the chair and heading into the front hall to grab the money. Ben follows close behind, a welcome little shadow—while Mira languishes between the living room and the hallway.

There's something striking about seeing someone you don't expect to see, and so Amy almost jumps when she swings the door open and recognizes Jeff Gamble from her World History class standing on the front step. He's got a red cap fitted snugly over his dark hair and a matching red jacket with *Bernardo's* printed in white cursive in the upper corner. The smell of cheese and onions rises up from the box in his hands, making Amy's stomach rumble. She'd been too busy studying for an English test during lunch to eat. Not that it made much of a difference. She's relatively certain the studying didn't do much good. Vocabulary has never been her strong point. It's not that she doesn't know the words; she does and she can use them in sentences correctly. It's the definitions that throw her— definitions that shift and slide and melt with context.

"Hey," says Jeff Gamble. Amy can think of only people she does not know particularly well by their first and last names. Like movie stars.

Familiarity has already flickered across his light brown eyes, which are set evenly against his dark skin. There's nothing more awkward than talking to someone you know, but do not actually know. Especially when that person is absolutely gorgeous. And he *is* gorgeous—with tender, moody eyes and a perfect jawline. The spitting image of Duane Jones in *Night of the Living Dead*. Amy would rather hold a conversation with her Valley girl cousins and their fake nails. At least she found comfort in their predictability.

"Hi," Amy replies, shifting her weight. The money crinkles in her palm, clinging to sweaty skin. Her stomach feels like it does when that swinging ship ride at the carnival lifts you up, right before you go back down again. Suspended in an unnatural, nauseating way.

Jeff Gamble gestures to the box. "It'll be nine ninety-nine."

"Right . . . yeah." Amy takes the pizza in one arm, shoving the cash out at him with her free hand. She doesn't count it. Doesn't need to. Eleanor makes sure to include an exact tip when she leaves money for takeout. Amy rubs her palm on the side of her skirt, glad the color of the skirt won't betray the sweat she's hiding.

"Having a good night?" Jeff Gamble asks, shuffling through the bills and securing them in his jacket. He slips his hands into the pockets of his jeans.

Amy nods, chest constricting. Tighter and tighter. Thinning each breath. She can feel the ship going down now, her insides swinging with it. Her vision tunneling because she can't find her balance. "S-sure. You?"

"It's all right." He shrugs amiably. Jeff Gamble plays football. And baseball. And soccer. And just about every sport you could imagine. A real jock. And while Amy doesn't have anything against him personally, she can't stand most of his friends. They're big and clumsy and loud. They talk without thinking, because they've never been expected to think, and coast by on athleticism and charm. Jeff is nice at least—smart and considerate—but overall, his crowd makes Amy's skin crawl. Her friends are all totally into them, which is just another reason she hasn't been spending all that much time with them lately. These girls—the one's she known since she was five—don't like Miles. They think he's a nerd and a loner. Maybe they are right, but Amy doesn't necessarily see this as being inherently negative. She never wanted to be *that* girl—the one who ditches her friends for a guy—but she's not the one ditching, is she? They're the ones keeping their distance. Judging her for dating

Miles. Drooling over the likes of Jeff Gamble and Dave Wallace. She actually used to have a crush on Jeff Gamble years ago, when they were in the fourth grade. She thought he had a pretty smile and liked how he always offered to help the teacher hand out papers. But that was when they were kids. And people change. Dave Wallace, for instance, used to be the real quiet type, even had a bit of a stutter. Golden hair and quiet blue eyes. Then he discovered sports. Fast-forward eight years and just last week Dave flipped Miles's lunch tray walking through the cafeteria. On purpose. Just because he could. Like one of the insufferable, over-the-top teens in *Carrie* who you think can't possibly be real except anyone who has been in high school knows they are.

So, this anxiety she's feeling in front of Jeff? Where is it coming from? Nowhere probably. She doesn't need a reason to be anxious; a panic attack doesn't need an excuse. She knows this by now, lives in constant fear of triggering one. That fear has become an unwanted tenant in her brain. She squeezes her free hand into a fist, then relaxes it slowly. She does this again. And again. And again.

Jeff Gamble is still loitering amicably on the front step. Waiting? Watching? Why the hell isn't he leaving? "Drive safe," she tells him, because she doesn't know what else to say. He looks down at Ben, who has remained close to Amy's side this whole time, and salutes him before offering Amy another smile and heading back down the front walk to his car, a little red sedan. Probably his dad's . . . or, no . . . his mom's. Jeff Gamble's parents are divorced, aren't they? Or maybe Amy is thinking of Jeff Carver. They're both in World History with her—*Honors* World History. Because she'd been too afraid to try to test into AP.

Amy closes the door and turns around. Air fills her lungs again like a balloon, swelling with relief. She shifts the pizza box, scorching hot against her arm, carefully into both hands as she leads the pack into the kitchen.

"Want to get some plates?" she asks Ben, putting the box on the island countertop. While he fetches paper plates from a creaky hinged oak cabinet above the dishwasher, Amy grabs the pizza cutter out of the drawer by the sink. In doing so she notices the magnets on the fridge, the way they are all situated in a full circle. "Cute," she says pointing to them.

"The ghost did that," Ben replies. The sound of his voice, which enters the air so sparingly, nearly gives her a start. "Anna Mae thinks it's the Cat Man, but it's a ghost."

Amy turns around, one hand on her hip and the other wielding the pizza cutter. "Who's the Cat Man?"

Ben shrugs.

Mira ruffles her brother's hair smugly. "Anna Mae is his girlfriend."

"No, she's not," he replies defensively, pulling away

Amy's brow knits. "And you think there's a ghost?"

Mira practically groans. "Oh, *please*. He's just making it up."

"The ghost lives here," says Ben, perfectly serious. "It moves things sometimes."

Right. A ghost. In an old house. Amy has seen enough scary movies to recognize a strange proclamation from a sweet little boy when she hears one and tries not to look spooked. It doesn't work and her eyebrows lift of their own volition. Kids aren't all that self-aware. That's what makes them creepy in movies. Their blatant innocence. Or the potential for the corruption of that innocence. The unexpectedness of its collapse. Why else would the Antichrist be such a popular movie trope? Ben isn't the creepy kind, though. He's not one of the children of the corn. And yet.

She can't help herself.

She has to ask.

"What kind of things?" Her tone is calm. Quietly, she reminds herself that Ben has never convinced a nun to jump off a roof or donned a clown mask to stab his sister. *He's a kid. A good kid. Not Damien Thorn. Not Michael Myers. A perfectly normal, good little boy.*

"The magnets," Ben explains casually, as if all houses are just a little bit haunted. "The cereal boxes. Toys."

Returning to the island in the center of the kitchen, Amy runs a hand gently through Ben's hair and places the pizza cutter next to the box. "Is it a nice ghost?" she asks, though the question seems pointless. Ghosts are never nice.

Poltergeist, The Shining, Thirteen Ghosts, Witchboard . . .

Would *The Amityville Horror* be considered a ghost story or strictly a demonic one?

The little boy shrugs.

Amy conjures up some cheap-as-plastic enthusiasm. "I'm sure it's a nice ghost."

The supernatural in general tends to be just as bad.

Worse, even. Chaotic and uncontrollable.

Don't Look Now, Carrie, Season of the Witch . . .

Amy plasters a smile on her face. Mira continues to watch the exchange like it's the spring musical and no one can remember their lines or hit the right notes. When Amy takes too long to move, Mira nudges the discussion along. "Can we eat?"

You watch too many movies, Amy tells herself—which is, of course, exactly what her father says all the time. It also happens to be the sort of thing someone *in* a horror movie says right before meeting their unfortunate demise.

That's the problem with loving scary movies. They put you on edge, but in these movies, it is *not* being on edge that gets people killed. Or possessed. Or driven completely insane by evil forces. Weirdly enough, scary movies are about the only things that don't trigger Amy's panic attacks. They never make her nervous or scared—a little jumpy maybe, but life does that plenty already. There's something safe about movies, knowing they're not real, and if she's seen them before, knowing exactly what's going to happen next. She takes comfort in that, more so than in anything else. She's sure this is why she wants to be a part of making them. There's a certain level of calculation—of certainty—that she relishes.

Trying really hard not to ask a thousand questions about the supposed ghost—Ben will get suspicious if she doesn't let it go—Amy flips open the lid of the pizza box and a rush of hot, oniony goodness swells in the air. Amy's the only one in her family who likes onions on her pizza, making this a treat. Onions seem to be the one thing she and Mira can agree on.

Amy recuts the slices so they are easier to separate and serves them out on the plates Ben hands her one at a time. "Kitchen or living room?" she asks, because Eleanor doesn't have a preference.

"Living room," says Ben. Mira doesn't argue.

"Awesome." Amy wants to encourage Ben when he voices an opinion on something. Anything. Eleanor warned her from the beginning that he can be passive. "He needs to know his ideas matter," she explained that first night. "I'm worried he's convinced himself they don't."

Grabbing the whole roll of paper towels off the counter, because she's *seen* these kids eat, Amy follows the pair back through the hallway. Both kids plop down on the couch, while Amy sits on the floor with her back against the base of the recliner so that she's closer to the table. She folds one ankle atop the other on the thick carpet. "Floor," Amy tells them before taking a big bite gushing with greasy cheese. Immediately she burns her tongue, cringes, and tries not to swear.

Mira and Ben stare.

"Come on," continues Amy, mouth half full. She pulls a paper towel off the roll and wipes her face before laughing. "You both have terrible aim," she says. "Butts on the floor. Heads over the table. Otherwise you'll get onions on the rug."

Reluctantly both oblige, and Amy blows on the pizza before taking another bite, this time getting a fair collection of shredded onions and seasoned cheese all in one mouthful. Her stomach gurgles approvingly.

Mira starts in on her own slice, while Ben pokes his sister and points to the paper towels and waits for her to hand him one before using it to absorb some of the grease off the top of his pizza. Amy finds the quiet precision of his caution adorable, but Mira glares at him irritably the whole time. Like he's embarrassing her—if Mira even cares enough what Amy thinks to be embarrassed.

Last time when they got pizza Mira said he only does this because he saw an old guy with a hat and a bow tie do it at a restaurant one time. "Because my brother is an old man," she'd lamented. Ten minutes later she was upstairs with a book, determined to keep out of the babysitter's sight.

They are the only kids Amy's ever sat for who don't ask her to turn on the television. She suspects it's because they've mentioned their mom watches a lot of television, the quiet thus being a welcome change. Amy's house was just the opposite growing up, so silent you could hear a fly land on the windowsill.

The kids eat contentedly, their fingers oily as they try to keep the hot cheese from sliding this way and that. Their plates become graveyards for lost onions. Splatters of sauce. Amy hands them each a few paper towels, then watches as they each get up to get a second slice. Ben even bashfully offers to get her one too. She tells him she would like that very much.

The kids go into the kitchen and return with their plates. Then Ben returns to the kitchen for Amy's slice, bringing it to where she is seated at the coffee table—a piece of furniture Amy thinks Eleanor brought from their old place. The wood is just a little darker than the rest of the wood and paneling on the first floor. "Thank you, cutie."

His words are small, bite-size, and polite. "You're welcome."

Eating in front of babysitters used to stress Amy out. She worried about making a mess, looking childish when she talked with her mouth full or feeling like a pig if she ate more than whichever modelesque, perfect teenage girl was sitting across from her that week. Neither Ben nor Mira seem to have this worry, but they still eat in a silence punctuated only by the occasional question from Amy about school. Ben responds to everything by shaking his head or nodding. Mira ignores the babysitter entirely—eating quickly, like the pizza might up and vanish if she doesn't finish it fast.

As they drift into silence again, Amy remembers what Ben said about a Cat Man. Did he mean it in a superhero way, like Batman? Or a movie monster way, like the Wolf Man? She opens her mouth to ask when she notices Mira slipping her fingers beneath that purple scrunchie, something she's been doing all night, and scratching at the skin with her nails. It could be poison ivy, but Eleanor would have said.

Her eyes drift to Mira's bruised knuckles and she frowns. Being a preteen girl shouldn't be so hard, but Amy knows, better than anything, that it always is. What's worse is that there's nothing she can say or do that will make Mira believe that she understands. That's the thing about being young—it's like every awful feeling you have is a brand-new sensation, never experienced by anyone before you. Poor Mira. She has so much to learn.

CHAPTER SIX

SIX YEARS AGO

Amy sat at the countertop, kicking her feet between the legs of the stool and running her fingers in straight lines across the surface of the dirty-looking off-white laminate. Back and forth. Back and forth. If her cousins were here, they would already have burned popcorn in the microwave and offered to do her homework for her in exchange for the combination to her parent's liquor cabinet. Instead, she had Sadie, who was presently heaving a large mixing bowl out of the bottom cupboard next to the dishwasher.

"Long division is better with snacks," explained Sadie, puffing out a breath as she put the bowl down next to the sink.

Amy wanted to resist the temptation to engage further, but all she'd had for dinner before her parents left was cereal. "What . . . kind of snacks?"

Sadie rested her weight on one slim hip. "How do chocolate chip cookies sound?"

"I don't know how to make those," she said at last.

"Well, fortunately for us I do, and if I teach you, then you can make cookies whenever you want. And how cool is that?"

It was cool. Especially since Amy's parents didn't buy sweets all that often. Ever, really. If she wanted donuts or M&Ms she had to wait until she was over at Whitney's house. Whitney didn't like junk food, but her dad kept the stuff stashed all over. Especially candy. Whitney's mom was always saying it was a wonder his teeth hadn't all fallen out, the way he loved chocolate. Only, Whitney and her dad were both tall and lean and everything Amy's body just didn't want to be. At the thought of this, Amy wrapped her arms—shamefully, protectively—around her own curves and gave Sadie the blankest of expressions. "We don't have chocolate chips."

Like some magical Madonna-inspired Mary Poppins, Sadie reached into the backpack nestled at her feet and pulled out a bag of chocolate chips. She narrowed her eyes with such exaggerated intensity that Amy could not help but giggle. "Always come prepared!" said Sadie, glancing about the room. "Now, we'll need flour, butter, sugar, eggs, and baking powder. Can you help me find those?"

Amy didn't know what to do. Sadie had a glow—an enthusiasm about her—that showed no signs of fading. So Amy slipped off her stool obligingly, prepared to do as she was told. Before she could reach the cupboard where they kept the sugar, Sadie stopped her, leaned back, and puffed out her cheeks like she'd just had the most earth-shattering notion.

"You are so pretty!"

Amy felt her breath catch. Pretty? Was she? No, of course not. Her mouth half opened, but she said nothing.

"I wish my hair was as thick as yours. It's gorgeous! You know, you would look super cute with bangs," Sadie continued, tracing a lock of Amy's hair with her fingers. "Have you ever thought about getting bangs?"

Amy shook her head.

"Well, if you ever want me to cut them for you—I gave my sister bangs last month and she absolutely loves them, gets all kinds of compliments. So, I can totally do yours if you want."

"I don't think my mom would like that."

Sadie's eyes glittered. "But would you like it? That's the question."

Amy swallowed hard, said nothing. Her excuse had been a convenient lie. Amy knew that her mother would probably consent, if Sadie was good at cutting hair and if it was what Amy really wanted. Only, the idea of doing something so drastic—so irreversible—made a balloon of panic rise in Amy's gut. She could feel herself getting nauseated. Dr. Somer had said these feelings were normal signs of an anxiety disorder. She told her they could work together on managing the feelings, but that was weeks ago and Amy hadn't been back to see her since. Her father didn't think there was anything wrong with her. "The girl is just oversensitive," he said the last time her mother had brought up seeing Dr. Somer again.

Amy gulped, desperate not to panic in front of her new babysitter.

Seeming to sense the girl's building apprehension, Sadie smiled. "You can look any way you want, peanut—be anyone you want." Her eyes were so bright as she spoke. So certain and optimistic in their conviction. "You got that?"

Amy nodded.

"Good. Oh—vanilla! Shoot. We'll need that too."

CHAPTER SEVEN

AMY

FRIDAY, OCTOBER 15, 1993
6:15 P.M. (5 HOURS AND 45 MINUTES BEFORE MIDNIGHT)

When the phone rings, Amy pops off the floor and hurries into the kitchen, assuming it's Eleanor calling to check in on the kids. Maybe her date was a bust. Or maybe she's having a good time and wants them to know she'll be out longer.

"Hello," she chimes upon pulling the receiver off its cradle on the wall, "Mazinski residence."

A fuzzy silence crackles.

"Hello?" she says again, this time a little louder. She hears something, possibly a snicker or a door closing, before the line goes dead. She waits for a moment, as if the line might resurrect itself. When it doesn't, she puts the phone back on the hook.

Creepy, yes, but not out of the ordinary, she reminds herself. Prank calls. Come October, they spread across Chase Hills like wildfire. Every year. Without fail. Small-town kids have nothing better to do with their time. Not that she can blame them for it. What else are they going to do? Go to the mall? Or the movies? Those things require money. And a car. And if you're under sixteen then you're just shit out of luck. So teenagers entertain themselves. Make prank calls and sneak out after dark and replace whiskey with water in their parents' liquor cabinet so no one will notice the bottle getting emptier and emptier. Amy has never done any of these things, but her cousins have. She's pretty sure Whitney has, too, not that she'd ever admit to it.

"Was that our mom?" asks Ben when Amy gets back to the living room. For the first time tonight, he looks eager. Alert.

"No, it was no one important." Amy shrugs nonchalantly, perhaps trying to adopt some of Eleanor's flare. Both Mira and Ben are seated where she'd left them, their dinner all finished. They are almost too well behaved to be real human children. "So, anyone have big plans for Halloween? It'll be here before you know it."

Mira cringes. "Our mom wants to dress up."

"Ooh, nice. What's her costume?"

"She won't say. It's always a surprise."

"Are you going to dress up?"

"People my age don't dress up," Mira states rather matter-of-factly. Amy tries not to laugh at the remarkably staunch seriousness in the girl's voice.

"I did, when I was twelve."

At this revelation Mira sighs, as if convinced that Amy has just offered definitive proof as to why she should not be dressing up.

Amy turns her attention to Ben as she sits again. "What about you?"

His head bobs up and down.

"What's your costume gonna be?"

"A . . . um . . . a TV."

"A TV?"

Again, his head bobs.

"That's . . . different."

"It's ridiculous," Mira interjects.

"No, it's unique." Amy comes to his defense. "I've never seen anyone be a TV before. You'll have to take pictures."

"We're gonna have a parade," says Ben.

"At school?"

He nods, his hands twisting bashfully. "You can come if you . . . if you want to."

"When is it?"

"Friday. At three."

"He means the Friday before Halloween," Mira clarifies.

Amy pretends to consider this, even though she knows she isn't watching the Miller's two-year-old until eight that night. She's never promised to show up outside of babysitting for one of the kids in the neighborhood before, but Ben tugs at something inside of her. Something small and fragile and broken—a piece of herself that always feels lacking. "I think I can swing that."

She smiles and he smiles back. Mira runs her forefinger along a dent in the coffee table. "That's weird."

"What's weird?" asks Amy.

"Going to a school parade when you don't have any kids."

Ben's face colors sharply—as if his sister has just endangered Amy's acceptance of the invitation. The babysitter shrugs. "You'll be there, won't you?"

"Yeah."

"You don't have any kids."

Ben giggles at this and Mira's finger falls from the coffee table as she brushes a flutter of hair away from her eyes. "Yeah, well, my mom's making me."

"Maybe my mom will make me too." Amy shrugs, throwing Ben a conspiratorial wink. His giggling erupts into full-on laughter, and Amy leans back, crossing one leg over the other. "Now, ladies and gentlemen, boys and girls, children of all ages—what else should we do tonight?"

The brother and sister shrug the same shrug, all high bony shoulders and blank faces. Amy noticed this the last time, too, the way they don't really know what to do with extended amounts of attention. Mira mostly shies away from it all together, while Ben just sits and waits, like she might lose interest. Or betray him. A little deer prepared to dart off into the night at the slightest disturbance.

"Board game? Movie? Dance-off?" Amy goes down a prepared mental list. The Dumont twins on Landon Street are really into Guess Who at the moment. It's the only thing that gets those girls to keep still, if only for half an hour. The Marvatto boy up on Milton Street, who's just turned nine, usually plays *Sonic* on his Sega for an hour and a half, then scares himself by watching *Are You Afraid of the Dark?* with the lights off. One time the Greenville Avenue Taylor girls, six and eight, begged Amy to watch the spooky Nickelodeon show, and their parents said it would be all right, so she let them, and the younger one, Missy, cried for an hour after it was time to go to bed. Terrified. Inconsolable. They haven't watched it since, of course, but that's all right. They've gotten relatively obsessed with *The Oregon Trail*. Or rather, Dina is obsessed and Missy sits and watches and always begs her sister not to shoot the rabbits because they are too cute and too small and too cuddly to eat.

The Mazinski kids, only a few houses away from the Bakers on Beacon Street, aren't into any of that; they don't have a Sega or a computer. Ben is definitely too young for *Are You Afraid of the Dark?*, and that brings Amy back to exactly where she started. Board games. Movies. Dance-offs.

"You have Guess Who?, right? And Rebound . . . Mousetrap, I think?"

Mira scrunches up her face and Ben examines the fibers of the carpet.

"Come on," Amy insists. "It doesn't sound like you want to read together. So let's explore our options. Besides, your mom is out. You should be living it up."

Mira winces. "Living it up?"

"Yeah! You know, eating too much sugar and watching scary movies."

Mira gives her a look, probably wondering why the babysitter is the one suggesting delinquent behavior. Amy practically lived off candy canes and horror flicks as a kid. Still does, really. Novelty foods and cheap thrills. Cheap thrills are the only kind of thrills that don't turn her into a hyperventilating disaster. That's what happens when it's life, *not* some movie, keeping you up at night.

"Can we go to bed?" asks Ben, those warm brown eyes soft and subtle. His fingers slide deliberately across the floor, likely comforted by the feel of the carpet. Sometimes Amy finds herself doing the same thing.

Amy's head cocks to the side. She steals a glance at the time on the VCR. It's not even six thirty. "*Come on*, guys," she groans. "Please. Do it for me. Do it for your mom. You think she wants you sulking bored all night?"

Ben bites down on his lower lip. Mira tosses her head back as if to ask the gods when this night will end. Before either can properly reject Amy's plea, the babysitter wipes her hands on her skirt and stands up. She narrows her eyes challengingly at Mira, just enough to pique the twelve-year-old's interest, and makes her way into the kitchen. When she returns, she's carrying Eleanor's boom box. She places it on the floor near the wall and plugs it in and turns the cassette deck on. Mötley Crüe's "Smoking in the Boys' Room" comes on, and even though the song's half over, Amy cranks the already high volume all the way up. Mira crosses her arms, her back firm against the base of the couch as Amy pulls Ben up to his feet and leads him by the hands to the other side of the coffee table. At first, he's reluctant to dance—rigid in his movements—but as she spins him around, a fissure of enthusiasm can't help but crack across the child's reserved exterior. She spins him again, this time farther out, and he giggles.

"This is degrading!" calls Mira over the roar of the music. Amy reaches out a hand for her to join them, but the girl refuses.

Amy and Ben continue to dance, tripping over themselves and laughing. Mira says over and over that the whole display is absurd, smirking with amusement only when she thinks Amy can't see. Amy swings her head back and forth, bouncing gently, and Ben tries to imitate her the best he can. She waves her arms dramatically. He waves his arms dramatically. Her head bobs. His head bobs. She scrambles her feet around real fast in a clumsily outrageous display, he scrambles his feet around real fast—nearly toppling over.

They join hands and swing around together, accelerating so fast they eventually pull apart. Ben tries to make up a few moves on his own, throwing his arms back and forth like some tiny little mosh-pit kid. Amy goes ahead and does the same, though she's certain he's doing a much better job than her.

The stereo is so loud that, at first, none of them hears the doorbell. When it rings again, Ben is the one to notice first, his feet coming to a halt and his gaze stalling as it falls across the front hall. Furrowing her brow, Amy turns and listens just in time to hear the third ring.

Hurrying across the room, she turns off the music by pulling the plug from the outlet and rushes to the door. She should check the window before opening it, but doesn't. Too eager, perhaps. Or maybe just too nervous.

Miles's face flickers when he sees her, not in the teen-love-puppy-dog way she hates, but as if his favorite song has just come on the radio. She wants to brush a loose, dark lock of hair away from his hazel eyes, but doesn't. The fussing would just make him self-conscious. "Busy?" he asks, acting like it's a joke even though an undercurrent of worry courses through it. He's concerned he's come at a bad time, which is charming in an awkward sort of way. Amy would likely be described as the confident one of the two, which says a lot considering she's relatively quiet and polite and even a little bit meek. A total nerd. But that's all right, because so is Miles.

"No," she says, worrying that her cheeks are red—her hair a little too frizzy from all the jumping. She's a terrible dancer—only ever dances with the kids she watches. Never with friends. Or Miles. "We were just, you know, rocking out."

Miles laughs softly, stepping into the doorway. His family moved to Chase Hills when he was fifteen, but Amy didn't have any classes with him until junior year. They both managed to score Mr. Mulvaney—the most merciful of the gym teachers—who gave the option of walking the length of the track instead of participating in soccer or softball or whatever sport was scheduled each week. Amy always opted for walking, as did Miles, and after enough days of circling the track in relatively close proximity, they began talking. He was considerate—mature, even—without being pretentious or smug. Every time Mr. Mulvaney blew the whistle Miles would kind of sigh—like he was disappointed that their time was up. He didn't ask her out though. Weeks went by and the more Amy liked him the more she was convinced she was just making their friendship up in her head, mistaking his politeness for actual affection.

Then one day, Miles's friend Barry came up to her during Photo II and begged her to ask him out. "He spends all of homeroom talking about you. How you're *so* smart and *so* pretty and *so* funny. This morning he went on and on about your laugh. Your *laugh*." Barry then proceeded to inform her that her laugh is not altogether impressive and that she should either put Miles out of his misery or go out with him already.

A guy had never shown any interest in Amy before, and it wasn't so much that he liked her laugh or that he thought she had a good sense of humor, it was that Miles thought she was smart. That's what drew her to him. No one had ever said this about her before—her parents maybe, but they didn't count. A few teachers, but saying that stuff was their job. Here was an actual boy respecting her mind. A boy. At sixteen. What kind of guy is into smart girls at sixteen? And he liked her body just the way it was. He didn't wish she was taller or skinnier or had better cheekbones. He was the first boy to ever call her pretty.

That afternoon during gym, she gathered her courage and asked if he wanted to hang out one day after school. Immediately, he said yes, and Amy felt a swell of pride, even if she had spent the half hour before gym on the verge of complete and unbridled panic. Three minutes after they got back into the building, she excused herself to the bathroom and threw up twice. But it didn't matter. She'd asked. And he'd said yes.

That's when the spiral began. She spent all week dreading and looking forward to and dreading the date again. She had to force herself to go through with it—but it was worth it. Miles makes her feel so very good. Calm. Normal. No—better than normal. He makes her feel like she is incredible because she is herself.

Lingering in the Mazinski doorway, Miles kisses her without asking, and he's only recently stopped asking. At Amy's insistence. Because she doesn't need the warning anymore. She loves the way his lips feel against hers, soft and nimble. The gentle press of his tongue between her teeth. Giddiness fizzes in her chest.

Gum! She forgot to chew gum after dinner. Sharply, she pulls away, hoping he hasn't noticed her onion breath. If he has noticed he doesn't say anything, staring deep into her eyes. Amy stares back, determined to keep a straight face, not to be that silly girl swooning over a guy. Except he makes it so easy, doesn't he? She feels like she could sink into those eyes, the ones that take her in with such care.

She looks down at the floor to compose herself, noting how one of the laces on his Vans is a little looser than the other. "I brought some tapes for later," she says. "For, you know, after the kids are asleep. If you're interested."

"Which ones?"

"*Night of the Living Dead* and *Halloween*."

He exhales in a soft, straightforward way that tells Amy all she needs to know. "Come on, really?" he groans, half wincing.

"Yes, really, they are good movies!" she insists, as if his confidence can be won through sheer willpower. Because for all the things she likes about Miles, for as well as he treats her, she absolutely can't understand what he has against scary movies. He complained for a week after she made him watch *Psycho IV* in August, but their biggest fight to date came just one month later, when he wanted to go to *Dazed and Confused* at this little indie theater and she wanted to see *The Good Son*. For three days they stopped speaking and, eventually, each ended up going to the movies alone. "You will like them. I *swear*."

"That's what you said last time," he reminds her gently. He is always gentle. Even when he's arguing. It might be one of her favorite things about him. "And *Halloween*? How can you even watch that? You're a babysitter."

She shrugs. "It's not like it's based on a true story.

"Are horror movies ever based on true stories?" Skepticism sits sharply in his hazel eyes.

Sweet, poor Miles.

Will he ever learn?

Amy stares at him like he's just called her by another girl's name. "Yeah! I mean, very loosely, but yeah . . . *Texas Chainsaw* . . . *The Exorcist* . . . *Amityville Horror*. But, seriously—just give *Halloween* a shot. It's all fake anyway. They filmed this thing on a super-low budget. They even had to reuse all the same leaves to make it look like fall everywhere. Isn't that funny?" She smiles, but he does not share her enthusiasm. Not even a little bit. She bumps his shoulder with hers playfully. "Come on. If you get scared, I'll let you put your arm around me."

Miles grins, leaning in to kiss her again before stopping short.

Amy's brow furrows. "What?" She turns around and sees Ben standing there in the hallway, his fingers wrung together and his chin tucked in just a little bit. There's a keenness to his expression that makes him look either very serious or fairly terrified—Amy can't tell which. "Hey," she says and smiles. "Remember Miles?"

Miles shoves his hands deep into his pockets. "Hey, there. It's Ben, right? You've got yourself a pretty awesome sitter here, Ben."

Ben does not look impressed that this stranger knows his name or says nice things about Amy, but Amy doesn't have time to put him at ease. Because there's a car door slamming in the driveway. It's too early for Eleanor to be back, and so Amy leans across Miles, stealing a peek down the side of the shrubbery-lined yard. Her brow goes very, very straight as her face tenses. Suddenly, she frowns. "Who's in your car?"

Miles pulls her back into the house, trying to situate himself more firmly between her and the doorway. "Listen . . . about that . . ."

"What?"

"Just . . . hear me out. Please don't get mad, okay?"

Amy folds her arms across her chest, leaning heavily on her left foot—away from him. Anxiety coils itself around her spine. "Why would I get mad?" Miles opens his mouth only to close it again. *"Why would I get mad?"*

As if on cue, Miles's brother, Patrick, shoots like a firecracker into the house, his arm crooked around the neck of Sadie, who's shooting right along with him like a gut punch. For a moment, Amy's stomach churns in a knot. She remembers Sadie well from the days when Sadie used to be her own babysitter. She's the type of girl who looks like she was crowned prom queen in high school . . . which she was. Sadie is pretty and vibrant and organized, with silky blond hair and luscious bangs. Her presence suddenly makes Amy feel smaller, like she's the one who is inferior. In need of coddling. Like a younger, plumper Carrie White standing next to good old Sue Snell. Suddenly she is struck by how small Chase Hills is and hates this place for it.

Patrick and Sadie make the most bizarre couple—the kind that would only work in a movie, because opposites never attract this hard

in real life. Patrick's T-shirt is rife with holes, as are his jeans—a stark
contrast to Sadie's perfection. If he was an extra in a movie, they'd cast
him as a creep in a bar or a would-be mugger.

Sadie smiles sweetly, almost conspiratorially, and waves at Amy on
their way in. She and Patrick head straight for the living room. If there's
a couch to be found, Patrick always knows where to find it. It's like an
instinct. A cheap, kick off your shoes, give no fucks to the world sense
of entitlement only harbored in the deep, calcified heart of suburbia.
Amy's anxiety rears, then settles, then rears again. She looks hard at her
boyfriend. "What are they doing here?" she hisses, not wanting Ben to
hear. Only, he's less than five feet away and can hear everything. And
whispering isn't really whispering when you're shouting.

"I—"

His response is cut short by Sadie's sister, Tess, as she drops her
weight against the doorway. "Hey there, Betty Crocker," she says with a
syrupy smile. Tess, never having bothered to learn Amy's actual name,
simply remembers her by the not-so-affectionate moniker. Tess is just
one year younger than Sadie, her hair curlier and thicker and darker
than her sister's, which amplifies the fact that Tess has the bigger per-
sonality, at least from what Amy can tell. It's not like the two have spent
a great deal of time together. Tess's grin melts into a pout, and she leans
in so close Amy can smell the stale blend of whiskey and fresh shampoo.
"Why so glum?"

Erupting in a fit of laughter, Tess rolls off the doorframe and follows
the others into the house. Amy just looks at Miles. "Their car broke
down," he explains hastily. "I wanted to drop them home, but they
wouldn't get out. I told them they weren't allowed over here, I did . . ."

Amy closes her eyes, rubbing her face as if she could scrub the whole
scene from her brain. When she looks at Miles again, he's wincing—
preparing for impact: the disappointed turn of her lips, an irrevocable
blow in his mind. He hates upsetting her. "Just—keep them out of the

kitchen, okay?" she says. "If they get hungry, order them pizza or some-thing. I don't want them eating Ms. Mazinski's food. And if they swear in front of the kids, and I mean *one single* expletive, all four of you are out of here, *understood*?"

Miles takes her hands in his. "Thank you."

When Amy turns around, Mira is standing there next to her brother, her brow knit. "Your friends are unappealing," she declares with un-paralleled certainty.

Amy steals a firm glance at Miles. "They are not my friends."

Mira looks hard at Amy, then at Miles, then at Amy again. With nothing more to say on the matter, she heads for the staircase. Amy feels for the girl. If it were up to her, she'd probably go hide too.

Ben doesn't follow immediately. He hesitates—a little undone in the wake of his sister's absence and tempted to stay—but the sound of Patrick cackling in the living room booms through the house. It sends something of a start through him—like ice cubes down his back. Eyes dark and complexion pallid, the boy quickly darts up the stairs after his sister.

Amy bites down on the inside of her cheek. "This is unbelievable," she mutters, closing the door behind Miles and dragging him into the living room. Patrick and Sadie are snuggled up on the couch, fawning over one another. Amy wants to scream, but won't. Because she does not want to scare the children. And because a tiny part of her still feels that Sadie will scold her if she acts out so egregiously.

Patrick's sneakers are on the coffee table, which is something he does at home, too, even though his mother can't stand it. Patrick is in his third year at County College, determined to put off actual adulthood for as long as humanly possible. Amy would identify with his plight if he wasn't such a monumental dick about it. Sadie, she's a junior at Drew University in Madison, a thirty minute drive from Chase Hills. She shares an apartment on campus with a few other girls, but spends a lot of time visiting her parents. Her dad had a heart attack over the summer and so she and Tess have been coming to help out a lot this semester during his recovery.

Sadie is the first to notice they've been discovered in the living room, nestling farther into Patrick's shoulder. "That little peanut you watch is cute," she notes with all the authority of a former babysitter. Amy used to idolize Sadie. She wanted to be just like her when she grew up, and now that she was mostly grown, she found it hard to wrap her head around the fact that Sadie was dating her boyfriend's brother. Of course, it wasn't nearly as hard to believe as the fact that Patrick and Miles are brothers in the first place.

Amy watches the way Sadie strokes the outline of Patrick's arm, tracing all the fine lines. Suddenly Amy is very aware of how far apart she and Miles are standing now that she's let go of his hand. The foot separating them is deep and vast. Can he feel it too—the cavernous space between them?

"What are you kids up to tonight?" asks Patrick, tossing his head back to half look at them. "You know, after the tykes go to bed." He raises an eyebrow suggestively at his brother, then nods in Amy's direction. Amy doesn't need to see Miles to imagine his cheeks turning red.

"Movies," Amy snaps, garnering the attention of both couch dwellers simultaneously. They smile identical smiles, as if their muscles are moving based on instructions from a single source. She'd heard that sometimes couples start to look alike, but she thought that was after years and years of marriage. Not eleven months of cruising around town and making out at the movies.

"Awww," coos Tess, her face scrunching up dramatically. "That's cute. Isn't that cute, Sade?" she says, pulling a small gunmetal flask from the deep pocket of her jacket and taking a swig.

Sadie mouths *ignore her* good-naturedly to Amy, who leans back on one foot, then the other.

About two weeks after they started dating, Miles invited Amy over for dinner to meet his parents—a milestone so unnerving that she actually stole a Xanax from her mother's bathroom to see her through it. This was close to Thanksgiving. Miles's mom and dad were perfectly nice. Very warm and considerate and wholesome. His mother kept saying how sweet Amy was, and more than once his father laughed graciously at Amy's awkward attempts at defense-mechanism humor. Patrick, who had told everyone he'd be there, never showed. No one seemed particularly surprised. Little did Amy know she'd spend the next year wishing he would bail on his family more often.

It's not just his attitude that's the problem—it's the way he demands things. Pushing and pushing until he gets his way. He's been pressuring Miles to make a move for months now. Amy knows this because Miles tells her everything, and while he plays it off like his brother is just some sex-crazed punk—which he *is*—she thinks deep down Miles is just as anxious as she is about the whole thing. After all, he's the one ignoring his brother's advice. He hasn't made a move. Even when it seems like he might, or even when Amy wants him to.

They've considered telling everyone they have done it, had sex, even though they haven't, just to take some of the pressure off. His friends are so shocked it's taking this long that they've started calling him Father Miles. Her friends . . . well, she hasn't really been talking to her friends enough to know what they think. Except for Whitney, who is convinced Amy is saving herself for marriage or "some weird shit" like that.

Tess extends her flask to Amy, who grits her teeth and waits for the others to start laughing. "Come on, Betty Crocker. A sip won't kill you." Tess sighs.

"I'm working," Amy says stiffly, sounding perhaps just a little bit full of herself. But it's true—this isn't her house and these aren't her kids. Even if she wanted to break a few rules, she wouldn't do it here. She was on the clock.

"What tapes do you have?" asks Sadie. She's always been good at pivoting, switching from one topic to the next with such attention and interest that everyone else cannot help but follow suit.

Amy readjusts her posture. "Slasher flicks." Of course, only one of them is technically a slasher film, but she doubts that any of her un-invited guests are going to argue semantics. Resting her weight on one foot, she tries to imitate the way Sadie pulls off politeness like a cute sweater.

Patrick looks back at his brother. "Don't you hate that shit?"

"I wasn't sure Miles was going to make it," Amy cuts in. "And I wasn't expecting anyone else to show up, so . . ."

Patrick winces. "Ouch, girl."

"What's your favorite these days?" asks Sadie, leaning across the couch and looking at Amy like they're the only two people in the room. Her eyes giddy and bright. Sadie remembers how much she loves movies. Sadie was always good at remembering things like that.

Amy hesitates. "I can't pick just one."

"Top three then."

"I guess . . . *Halloween*, *The Hitcher*, and . . . *The Curse of the Cat People*."

Patrick's expression twists. "Isn't that the one where the guy's trying to fuck his sister?"

"You're thinking of the *Cat People* remake," she replies. This has always been the difference between her and her cousins. Charlie and Donnie like the really gory stuff—and she does, too, but she also finds the super classics to be just as compelling. Haunting in a very unique, specific way. "The original is from the forties," she continues. "And *The Curse of the Cat People* is its sequel."

She's always considered it to be a strange coincidence that Oliver and Alice's daughter in *The Curse of the Cat People* is named Amy. Perhaps what's even more uncanny is that the child, played by Ann Carter, is a quiet little daydreamer. Ann Carter's Amy is so sweet and so kind and tries so hard to be what her parents want her to be. She tries to make them proud, but she is who she is—and eventually they realize that they should be supporting her instead of trying to change her. Amy's always been just a little bit jealous of Ann Carter's Amy in that respect. That child is so loved. That's not to say that Amy feels unloved exactly, just—distant. Apart. Out of step with everyone else on the dance floor. Lately, though, Ben has begun to remind her of Ann Carter's Amy. They have the same soulful, glittering eyes—filled with thoughtfulness and curiosity, and perhaps a little sadness too.

Is he too young to watch a movie like that? It's not like the film is terribly violent or anything—not like some of the movies she saw at his age, with masks made out of human skin and buckets of blood and head-twisting possessions.

"Oh, and *Amityville*!" Amy adds hastily. Everyone looks at her blankly. She shrugs. "It's a classic."

When Amy was fifteen, she and Donnie got into a rather heated debate about Jack Nicholson and James Brolin. Donnie thought Nicholson in *The Shining* gave the best madman performance of all time. Amy, on the other hand, insisted that Brolin's subtler transformation in *The Amityville Horror* was more striking. The argument got so intense that Donnie broke a lamp and Amy managed to swear more in those fifteen minutes than she had in the entirety of her life leading up to then. Her other cousin—Donnie's brother, Charlie—could have been the tie-breaker, but he thought the both of them were wrong. He believed Sissy Spacek was better in *Carrie* than Nicholson and Brolin combined. Donnie and Amy quickly united to turn on poor Charlie, mostly because he was right. Not that Amy would ever admit it. She is, if nothing else, fiercely loyal to her most beloved fictional characters.

"Which is the one that was just out? The one with the Ouija board?" asks Patrick, head cocked to one side.

"*The Devil's Doorway*?"

"Yeah," he laughs. "That was shit."

Tess throws him a look. "No it wasn't—"

"If it was shit then why'd you see it?" asks Amy.

Patrick shrugs, which is his way of saying that he was too drunk at the time to remember.

The Devil's Doorway, which had a great color palette and absolutely no vision, was actually the sequel to *Witchboard*. Amy thought the second film was just all right, but really liked the camera angles and the story from the first one. Her mom laughs when she gets all practical in dissecting horror movies. She doesn't see how anyone can take them seriously.

"So, are you making Miles take you to the Haunted Corn Maze?" says Sadie, directing the question at Amy.

Releasing a breath steadily through her nose, Amy shakes her head.

"Really?" Tess raises an eyebrow. "I heard it's a scream."

Patrick looks at her. "Yeah? From who?"

"Ava and Jake," says Sadie.

"They went last weekend," Tess adds. "Their dad gets free passes because he knows the guy who runs it."

Amy doesn't say anything, unwilling to draw attention to herself. Or the fact that she hates haunted house attractions. And corn mazes. And pretty much anything that exists in the real world. They make her dizzy with panic. Movies are controlled—carefully constructed and unalterable narratives. In real life things can get messy—not in a guy's intestines hanging out way, but in unexpected ways. There's no control out in the world. There is only life. Chaos.

"Should we check it out?" asks Patrick, pulling Sadie close.

She smiles in that bashful, sexy way Amy wishes she could emulate. "Absolutely."

"Who wants to watch *Halloween*?" asks Miles suddenly. He must be trying to make amends, because he'd rather pull his own fingernails out one by one than watch the damn movie.

Patrick scowls. "That horseshit?"

"Well, you can always leave." Amy poses the idea to the room, intentionally avoiding Patrick's gaze. A slab of silence follows, awkward in its bulkiness. Crowding the already confined space.

"I told you she'd be mad," Sadie chimes knowingly, shifting away from Patrick and picking at a hangnail.

Patrick sighs. "Virgins are always mad."

Tess muffles a burp of a laugh. Sadie swats at his arm disapprovingly. Amy must have made a face, because Patrick pouts at her. "Aw, Ames? What?" he says. "Did I say something wrong?" The charm in his voice is sticky and gritty and stale. He likes to push her buttons because it's so easy. Because it requires so little effort—no effort really. Her frustration is just a by-product of him being who he is and what he is and where he is all at the same time.

But who does she want to slap more right now? Patrick for existing? Or Miles for bringing him here? Amy can't decide. And so she forces a smile, one as stiff and fraudulent as it is uncomfortable. "Never," she says, not even trying to sound like she means it. She steals a quick glance at Miles, whose eyes are pleading with her not to lose it. She starts scooping the discarded paper plates off the coffee table. "I've got to wrap up the pizza," she mutters before fleeing the room, her brain on the verge of boiling.

In the kitchen she takes in a deep breath, which quakes and quivers as she releases it again. The emptiness of the room does provide some comfort, and when she brings in another breath, she is able to let it go with a little less fragility. She throws the plates and the paper towels in the garbage, then proceeds to squeeze and relax her hands.

One.

Two.

Five times.

When she's done, she inhales through her nose, exhales through her mouth, and flips open the pizza box. Calmly, she retrieves a roll of tin foil from the drawer by the sink, and she's halfway through tearing off a sheet when Patrick comes in, hands nestled deep his pockets all nonchalantly. Like he wants to make peace. Only Amy knows better than to buy it. Because Patrick only knows how to wage war.

Pretending to ignore him, she places two slices of leftover pizza on the foil and folds the edges all around.

"Let me ask you something," he starts, leaning against the island. He picks a sticky piece of loose cheese out of the box and pops it in his mouth, an act that leaves a little smudge of grease along the corner of his lip. "If you're so obsessed with movies, why do you watch kids? Shouldn't you be working at Moore's or something instead of this shit?"

Moore Video. The owner, Elias Moore, is remarkably fond of pizza. Amy's in there all the time. Browsing. Renting. Suggesting movies to other people roaming the stacks. She actually tried to get a job there last year. That was maybe a few weeks before she and Miles started dating. She likes Mr. Moore. He reminds her of Mr. Rogers in a sweater-clad, neighborly sort of way. He would have been glad to hire her if he could, but she's underage, and employees can't be underage because they'd be handling the adult videos in addition to everything else.

She doesn't tell Patrick this, though. He'd only get a kick out of it. Start asking if she's ever been in the dirty-movie aisle. She hasn't, but she doubts he'd believe her.

Stiffly, Amy continues to crease the curves of the foil even though the edges are about as tight as they are ever going to be. Her silence only fuels him. "Come on, Ames." He pouts, or at least she's pretty certain he's pouting. He thinks it makes him look charming, and maybe it does just a little. But only because when he does it, he resembles Miles, and Miles is charming without meaning to be charming. Sweet without realizing that's what it is he's being. She tells herself dealing with Patrick is a small price to pay for him, even if lately it's felt like the price has been steadily increasing. Inflation. What a bitch.

Amy balls up her fists and relaxes them again, sharply meeting his eye. "Miles was caught shoplifting last week."

She half expects him to react to the information in a genuine way—shrug his shoulders and smile some disgusting smile and say guilty as charged—but he doesn't. He just stands there. And stares. And waits for her to explain the accusation.

Her hands constrict and loosen. Constrict and loosen. "Are you telling me you didn't stick a Milky Way in his pocket?"

"Maybe he was hungry."

"He's allergic to chocolate."

"What can I say? Baby bro likes to live on the edge."

"You are always doing this."

"Doing what?"

"Pulling this shit on him!"

She regrets saying this almost immediately, because his eyes are gleaming. He sees getting her to swear as a personal point of pride. Because he likes it when she swears. And she's always been determined not to give him the satisfaction of doing anything he likes.

"You know he is a decent human, right? And you—you're just determined to screw that all up."

"If he's so great maybe you should, you know, *show* him."

She curls her hands into fists—squeezes—and loosens them again. She'd always thought her anxiety was what kept getting in the way of her and Miles having sex, but lately she's started to worry that it's because of Patrick and his damned persistence. He keeps nudging. And insinuating. She can't let Patrick win, though, even if it means she loses in the process. The stern, solid line of her mouth trembles. "You're an asshole."

He nods agreeably. "True. But really, any other girl would at least have given him a hand job by now. I mean for Christ's sake, what are you waiting for? An invitation?" He grins cartoonishly—almost like a super-villain. "Because I'm sure he's *given* you an invitation, if you know what I mean."

Amy tilts her head. She doubts Miles has told his brother anything about what they have and have not done. "Don't tell me how to use my body," she says, looking Patrick up and down with a sneer. "You probably don't even know how to use yours." She slams the pizza box shut, taking the wrapped-up leftovers to the fridge. Shoving a pack of cheese to the side, she puts the pizza on the second left-hand shelf. When she turns back around again Patrick is standing on her side of the counter, so close she nearly jumps. He smells like bad cigarettes.

"You know he's thinking about you when he jerks off anyway," says Patrick.

Amy's nails dig into her palms.

It's his turn to look her up and down distastefully. "Not that I can understand why."

She pushes him, gently but with enough force to put some space between them. He laughs. The only thing better than a swearing Amy is a confrontational one. The babysitter walks around to the other side of the kitchen—her breathing rapidly increasingly—but he keeps on chuckling.

"You really are a little fucking Girl Scout, aren't you?"

Amy spins around, her heels digging firmly into the floral linoleum. "You're an asshole. You've always been an asshole," she hisses, her voice low. Because there are the kids to consider. And Miles. And because if she starts to shout now, she's not sure she'll know how to stop. "You'll always be an asshole. In fact, you are *such* an asshole that the world can't possibly be big enough for any more assholes! God, you're such a waste of—"

Whatever insult she's about to conjure evaporates instantly as the floor creaks behind her. Terrified that Miles has come in to see them fighting, relief settles between Amy's shoulders when she sees it's only Sadie. She's got this bemused look on her face—like she's just walked into the men's bathroom by accident. She tilts her head. "Am I interrupting?"

Patrick intentionally bumps Amy as he goes over to Sadie, wrapping his arms around her waist and planting a gratuitous kiss on her lips—one with more tongue than seems at all necessary to get the job done.

"Your brother wants to talk to you," Sadie says to him when at last they pull free of one another. Patrick slips a second, more tender kiss against her cheek. Then he throws one more toothy grin at Amy before sauntering out.

Sadie waits and then, favoring one hip, crosses her arms. "You're welcome."

Amy only responds mutely, vaguely. Sadie is too smart to be with Patrick. Prom queen *and* valedictorian in high school. A straight-A student on dean's list every semester now.

"I take it you and Miles still haven't . . ." Sadie is tasteful enough to let the implication fall quietly between them.

Amy pretends to glance out the window over the sink, though the shades are drawn and even if they weren't it would be too dark out there to see beyond her own reflection.

The silence lags. Amy takes in a breath, holds it tight, and returns her attention to Sadie—who is still staring not at or beyond, but straight *through* her with the precision of a scalpel. Sadie's green eyes flex. "Why not?" she asks, arching a thick but carefully tweezed eyebrow. The words aren't unkind. In fact, they are sympathetic. Genuine.

Amy shrugs. "What makes you think we haven't?"

"Pat doesn't know everything, even if he thinks he does, but he's usually not wrong about this stuff."

"This stuff is none of his business."

"You know that and I know that—even Pat knows it. But that won't stop him. As long as he thinks he'll get a rise out of you, he'll keep at it."

"And that doesn't bother you?" barks Amy, steeling herself and looking Sadie directly in the eye. The phone begins to ring, but she refuses to break away from Sadie's gaze. "He's controlling and selfish and a bully and that just doesn't bother you?"

She can't understand it. She never would have imagined her sweet, gentle Sadie with a guy like this. Not in a million years. Sadie takes in a breath, frowns, and exhales sadly. "No."

The phone doesn't let up. Amy's blood boils and curdles and dries up inside her veins. Her entire circulatory system is on the verge of crumbling into ash. Her teeth clench down hard. She grimaces. "Why not?"

The ringing phone goes silent. "Nobody's perfect," says Sadie.

Amy would argue that there's a huge difference between imperfect and intolerable, but she doesn't. Instead, her voice goes quiet and she pretends to examine the floor. "How's your dad doing?" she asks.

Sadie's expression doesn't change. "Fine."

"My mom says she talked to yours at the grocery store last week," Amy continues. "She said it's been really hard on you and Tess—"

"It is what it is," Sadie cuts her off, not sharply but with a certainty that implies the conversation will go no further than this. And it won't. Amy used to confide in Sadie all the time when she was little, but Sadie never returned the confidence. No. Sadie always played things closer to the chest than that.

Amy looks at the clock on the stove. Just to look away. And when she looks back again Sadie crinkles her nose. "You'd look better with bangs," she says in what feels like a tender attempt to change the subject, one that harkens back to the days when Sadie was looking out for her. Maybe, in her own way, she still is. "Do you want me to cut them for you?"

CHAPTER EIGHT

BEN

"Why is Amy so mad?" asks Ben, pressing his bare toes against the wooden base of his sister's bench. It's at the foot of her bed, filled almost to bursting with stuffed animals and toys—not that she would ever admit it. She pretends she doesn't care about them anymore, but she does. Except for Crissy, who talks sometimes in the middle of the night. It gives both of them the creeps. Crissy was Mom's doll when she was a kid, which is why M can't get rid of it—only hide it. The same way you'd bury something you don't want anymore in the ground. He can't even remember what the doll looks like, but he still knows her high little voice. Just the thought of it sends a shiver down his back. If he had to choose between the ghost and Crissy, he would choose the ghost.

Ben straightens the clunky, yellow plastic flashlight on the floor between his knees and presses the button on the top. A little circle of light appears against M's bench. He turns the dial on the right-hand side and the light turns red.

He looks up, assuming his sister has heard him. Or is pretending not to have heard him. She leans a pen against her lips thoughtfully, then scribbles a few more lines in her notebook. "Who cares," she mutters, scratching the inside of her left wrist as she writes. That's the wrist she usually wears a scrunchie on to hide the red marks, but she took it off when they got upstairs. She must be annoyed. She's been scratching all night and she only scratches like this when she's annoyed. It pinkens her skin and makes the green and blue veins beneath appear gray.

"They were yelling a lot," he continues, though yelling doesn't seem like the right word. Shouting would be more like it. And he's pretty sure he heard Miles storm out of the house too.

Ben lifts his chin up a little in an attempt to see over the bottom of the bed, but all he can spot is his sister's pale green comforter, slightly ripped in one corner and loose at the seams. She wants a water bed more than anything right now, but Mom says they are too expensive. M throws up on long car rides anyway, so he doesn't know how she'd even stand a water bed, with it rocking back and forth all the time. Aunt Patty has a water bed, though. If M could be anyone in the world, she'd want to be Aunt Patty, who doesn't have kids to take care of or bad boyfriends to disappoint her. "What are you writing?" he asks.

"None of your business."

Ben doesn't know if she uses the book as a diary or just for doodling. M never shares any of her stuff with him. He turns the dial. Red again. "Do you think they broke up?"

"What?"

"Amy and Miles. Do you think they broke up?"

Still preoccupied with her pen, M kicks her feet back and forth lazily. "I don't know. Maybe," she mumbles, losing interest. He can tell because her voice gets all soft and low when she's no longer paying attention. "Why do you care?" she asks suddenly, putting the pen inside the notebook as a bookmark and slamming the cover shut. The question catches him off guard. Her eyes fix on him, bright and steady. She probably already has an answer picked out, only she wants to hear him say it.

Ben shrugs vaguely, which only feeds the suspicion nestled in the lines of her face. He changes the color one more time, but it only goes back to the beginning. He turns the flashlight off and pretends to be distracted by the posters on her wall—all for music he doesn't listen to and probably never will. Jimi Hendrix. The Rolling Stones. Mom's all about the eighties, but M—she's an old soul, like Mom says. She's in love with everything that came before them. Before Mom. Aunt Patty, who they call aunt even though she isn't an aunt, is the one who got her into the Rolling Stones. Patty likes to say she and M are both *kind-ed spirits*, whatever that means. He doesn't really like the Stones. Mom says their hair was *too posh in the sixties*, which is another phrase he doesn't understand, but he's pretty sure he doesn't like *posh* either. But M must.

That's how different they are—him and M. They can't agree on the same music or movies or games. They don't like any of the same foods—he hates onions on his pizza even though he's never said as much, because M won't eat it any other way. He likes strawberry-flavored everything and she prefers blue-raspberry-flavored everything. It's the same with chocolate and vanilla. He likes all his classes at school. She hates every single one of them. Even language arts, which she's really good at. She sleeps with the lights off. He'd keep them all on if he could. He's right-handed. She's left-handed. She looks like Mom, he looks like—well—no one, really.

The only thing they have in common is the Fear. That's what he calls it, anyway. Because it's big enough and scary enough to be set apart from any old fear with a lowercase *f*. They've always been afraid—the both of them. Inexplicably. Afraid of losing. Afraid of being left behind. Going back to the way things were. Isn't this how all brothers and sisters go? Different every which way and yet so very, very much the same.

Ben wonders what his sister calls it, if she calls it anything at all, but he's never asked. The Fear isn't something they talk about. It's like a pact they made a long, long time ago. One they've sworn not to share with anyone. Including each other. Maybe that's why they're so different when it comes to fighting the Fear—trying to chase it away. Ben wields questions like a sword—believes that questions will lead to answers, and answers will protect him. M, she wraps herself up in anger. Takes comfort in it. Uses it to distance herself from anything and everything that might try to knock her off balance. Because it's hard to focus on the Fear when you're too busy raging. And M, she's good at raging. Just like Mom. And Dad. Where is Ben's rage, then? Is it lying dormant somewhere, waiting to be awoken? Or is it his missing part—the thing that makes him different from his parents and his sister?

"Did you mean what you said?" asks Ben, looking back at her warily. "That Mom won't be back before we go to bed?"

"When has she ever been back from a date before two in the morning?"

"Is she on a date?"

"Seriously?"

Ben stares. There are lots of reasons she could be out, right? For work or with a friend. Only she doesn't work nights anymore. And she doesn't really have any friends in this town. He frowns. It doesn't have to be a date. It could be something else. She could just be going somewhere different.

"It's a date," M assures him dryly, as if having read his thoughts. Sometimes Mom talks about getting them a new dad—finding a good one who will treat them right. Ben thinks he would like that, but M can't stand the idea of it. She says men are bad—all men—and one day he will grow up and be bad too. He doesn't know how. And she won't tell him either.

When they'd first moved into the house Mom didn't really seem interested in going out with anybody. She was too busy getting them settled and making sure M and him had all the right clothes and notebooks and backpacks for school. Then some guy she met at the mall asked her out, and she said yes. Mom got them a babysitter—Amy, whom one of the other moms at his school had recommended—and went out to dinner with the mall man, and M was so mad she hardly said anything all night. Ben doesn't like Mom leaving, but he does like Amy. He keeps hoping Mom will invite her over and stay, but so far, she's only ever had Amy here to watch them when she's gone.

Ben doesn't remember whether Mom dated a lot after they left their dad. M says she did, but Ben only remembers the parties she used to throw at the apartment. They are thick and cloudy in his mind—blended together like a milkshake. All those people over late at night, smoking what they said weren't cigarettes and drinking lots of beer and laughing more than he'd ever seen anyone laugh at anything. Mom doesn't have the parties anymore, which M should like because she hated those parties. But apparently Mom going out on dates is just as bad. He doesn't know why. M seems sure of it, though, and he agrees with her. He doesn't like Mom being out on a Friday night. Especially since it means they're stuck in the house all night long. And with the Cat Man out there—no, his mezuzah pendant will protect him. He squeezes it to his chest. The one by the front door should protect M and Amy, but what about Mom? She doesn't have one with her.

"We don't go to temple anymore," he says softly.

M glances up at him. "You remember that?"

Ben nods, even though he doesn't remember much about when Mom used to take them. There's a feeling about it, though—buried deep inside him. A sense of missing it. He can sort of recall the hum of the songs, and how they made him feel safe. Warm. Like lullabies in the bathtub.

"She only took us there because she couldn't pay the rent and the super turned the heat off."

Ben's head bends to one side. He doesn't know what a super is, but he does know how important it is to have heat, especially in the winter.

"You don't remember, do you?"

"I remember," he mumbles, even though he doesn't. And she knows that he doesn't.

M sighs. "It was the middle of January, so she'd take us to the diner the rest of the week and temple on Fridays. They had free food."

The table set up after services. Cookies and cakes. Mom let them have dessert for dinner. That part he does remember. Little chocolate brownies. Fudgy with thick, creamy frosting. "But we could still go, couldn't we?"

"Why?" M replies. "Mom doesn't believe in God."

"Yes, she does."

"No, she doesn't. There's no foundation for God. Just books that say he exists. How do you know the people who wrote those books weren't lying? Or telling a story? That's all books are anyway. Stories."

Ben turns the mezuzah around his neck between his fingers. "Do you have to believe in God to go to temple?"

"Obviously."

Ben frowns, deciding here and now that he believes in God. Even if Mom and M don't. He squeezes the pendant tight in the palm of his hand. M's eyes shift across him. He can feel it. Sometimes he's absolutely certain she has a key to his brain. She waits until he isn't paying attention and then uses it to unlock all his secrets. It's the only way to explain it—how so much of the time she reacts to something he's thought before he's had a chance to say anything.

Rolling off the bed, M hops onto the floor and goes to the desk in the corner of the room. The desk came with the house. There are a few slim books propped up on it against the wall. She plucks one off and throws it at her brother on her way back to the bed.

"There," she sighs, falling back onto the comforter. The mattress creaks like it's about to bust a spring. Ben looks at the cover of the book. *Number the Stars.* He doesn't need to read the titles to remember all of M's books. He knows what the covers look like. A few M stole from the library, the rest were all Chanukah presents Nana sent them. This one was a present. "That's what it's like to be Jewish," she insists.

Ben stares down at the face of the girl on the cover. She's staring right back at him. She looks serious and wise and sad. Mom refuses to read this book to him. Says he's too little. That's usually her excuse for a lot of things. He tried reading it himself one time, but there were just too many big words on too many pages.

Ben continues to hold the book in his lap, watching as his sister returns to her scribbling.

"Quit staring already," she mutters irritably.

"I'm not," he replies, and when she looks up at him, he turns his attention to the book, tracing the letters in the title one by one.

"Liar."

A frown curdles on his face.

"Do you know what happens if you stare when you shouldn't be staring?"

He outlines the title of the book again, shaking his head without a word.

"You turn to salt!"

Ben looks up. "That's stupid."

"No, it's not."

"You're wrong."

"I'm never wrong."

"You're lying."

She shrugs. "It's in the Torah. Just ask Mom. This husband and wife named Lot and Idit were leaving a bad place and they weren't supposed to look back at it and Idit did anyway and she turned into a pillar of salt."

"Why?"

"Because looking back was wrong. And so she was punished for it."

"But why salt?"

M's eyes narrow. "I don't know. I didn't write the Torah. Ask a rabbi. They know all about those things."

Ben doesn't know any rabbis. He doubts M does either.

He thinks about what it must be like to turn to salt. Is it like exploding? Or burning? Or is it like magic—one minute you're a person and the next minute you're salt? He can't even imagine what a person's worth of salt would look like. It's probably like what they put on roads in the winter—those big bags people pour on the sidewalk. To melt the snow. What if those bags aren't filled with salt at all? Just people who were bad and punished for it. This idea terrifies Ben and so he tries to think of something else. Anything else.

"Will Amy check on us?" he asks suddenly. He wants to see her again before she leaves—before his parade. She might get mad, though, if she comes up here and sees that they're still awake. And that he's not in his room.

M looks up again. "Do you ever shut up?"

This is her go-to line. Fortunately, Mom told him exactly what to do when M says this to him. He smiles big—so big his lips hurt—and shrugs innocently like a perfect little angel. "No."

M's expression sours. "Last time she came halfway up the stairs around midnight," she admits reluctantly. "So as long as we're quiet, she'll probably, you know, do that. If you're up she won't know. Not unless you tell her. Do you plan on telling her?"

He shakes his head and a twinge of worry gnaws at his gut. Mom wanted him in his own room half an hour ago, but he's still here watching M write in her notebook and kick her feet and pretend to be older than she actually is. M is the only one who can ever get him to do things he's not supposed to be doing. She doesn't trick him or bully him into it either. He does what M says because he wants to please her, to be granted admission into her super-secret-too-cool club of one.

There's a knock from downstairs suddenly, the front door maybe. A loud one. Ben stiffens—immediately alert. *Mom!*

Scrambling to his feet, he scurries out of the room before M can stop him. Before she can even call his name. Because Mom's come home. Finally. There's the sound of more knocking.

He rushes to the stairs, M trailing close behind as he comes to a sudden stop on the landing. He watches as Amy opens the front door, feels the weight of his own heart sinking as his mother's face does not appear on the other side of it. No—it's the face of a man. A man Ben can't quite place.

He watches Amy watch the man, who notices Ben and Mira on the stairs and winks suddenly. Ben feels his cheeks flush.

"Can I help you?" Amy says, sounding a little unsure of herself.

The man at the door grins. "I don't know. Can you?"

CHAPTER NINE

AMY

The smell of pepperoni, slightly burned, moves in waves across the living room. A gentle sea of roasted flesh. It's making Amy more than a little nauseated, but she says nothing as she sits in the big recliner, hunched so far over her history book the damn thing might very well swallow her whole. She probably wouldn't mind it either. Even if it spits all her guts right back out again *Nightmare on Elm Street*–style. It would almost be a relief.

It is hard to disappear.

But only if disappearing is what you want.

Stealing a glance at Miles, she realizes he's staring at her—has probably been staring at her since his brother's pizza arrived. Jeff Gamble hadn't showed up this time—it was some delivery kid from another school district who stammered and laughed too much when Tess told him she liked his jacket.

The second pizza was more than necessary. It had only taken Patrick fifteen minutes in the Mazinski house before he started rummaging through the fridge in search of scraps. The very fact that Miles had not foreseen this predicament bothers her more than she's particularly interested in admitting.

Miles smiles—likely hoping to fix the damage done—and Amy quickly turns back to her textbook. If the Mazinski house is haunted, she'd prefer the ghost to make itself known already and send her unwanted guests screaming.

After they ordered the pizza, Tess went and plugged the boom box back in. Turned it way up. Mötley Crüe has been blaring at full volume for what feels like forever. Twice now Amy has asked them to turn it down. They haven't listened. And every time she goes over and adjusts the volume herself, Patrick manages to slip across the room to turn it back up again. At least the kids aren't in bed yet, so it can't wake them. Or are they? Ben had asked about going to bed over an hour ago. Maybe he's already tucked himself in.

Amy hurriedly flips through the last three pages of chapter 5, not quite sure if she is retaining any of the information between the pepperoni and the music. Slamming the book shut, she shoves her school stuff into the backpack, closes the zipper, and rises. Miles stands with her, almost on ceremony. Like a goddamn knight. Amy turns away to avoid him, scratching a dry elbow and then fiddling with her ring. She knows that he knows she hasn't been speaking to him on purpose, just like *he* knows that *she* knows it's worrying him.

All at once Amy realizes she's grinding her teeth—not from the pressure in her jaw but from the dull throbbing it has spawned at the base of her head. Her father hates it when she grinds her teeth. Says it's an unattractive habit in a person. Of course, it's a habit Amy learned after watching him do it for years. She never accuses her father of hypocrisy, though—no, she just waits until he leaves the room and then goes back to grinding her teeth even harder. Blending passivity and avoidance, that's how she deals with her father. With everyone. Wait until they go away. Wait until they leave her alone. Wait and wait and wait and wait until the earth gives way beneath her and she slides into the deep, dark nothingness in all its infinite glory. Only, she doesn't want to just sit around doing nothing at the Mazinski house. Not with the kids upstairs. She wants her unwelcome houseguests to show a little courtesy. A little decency.

Marching over to the boom box, Amy reaches down and pulls the plug out of the wall so forcefully the outlet sparks. Silence punctures the room. In one fluid motion, all eyes turn to her.

"What the hell?" Patrick barks, throwing his arms up.

Amy's jawline trembles. Her teeth are so tightly clenched she's likely to crack a tooth. "It was too loud," she tells him with a stale, overworked smile. She falls back into her chair and crosses her arms innocently. "It'll bother the kids."

Tess laughs. "Judging by their mom's taste in music, I think they're used to it being loud."

"It won't matter."

"I bet she's hot," says Patrick, his fingers dancing across Sadie's left knee.

Sadie grins, her lips drawn in close to his like Patrick is hiding a magnet between his tongue and his teeth. "You *do*, do you?"

"Miles says she doesn't look like a mom," Patrick replies, watching Sadie's lips part in a practiced and particular kind of way, like she's getting off on drawing him close. Distracting him.

At the mention of his own name, Miles's head quickly sinks between his shoulders. His gaze darts to Amy for fear that she is going to be even madder at him now. Only, Amy actually agrees with Patrick on this one and so she says nothing—only grimaces.

"Hey!" Patrick jolts up, like some tiny lightbulb in his head just went off. "Hey—hey—hey, maybe this Mazanki chick is the one who's been, you know, breaking in everywhere—stealing people's shit!"

"Mazinski," Amy corrects him.

Patrick shrugs. "Whatever." He tosses his brother a look for support. "Didn't you say they moved here a few months ago? That's when the looting started!"

"It's not looting," Amy says before Miles can get a word in. "And Ms. Mazinski isn't doing anything illegal."

Patrick rubs his thumb across a hole in the knee of Sadie's stocking. "I don't know. You've watched her kids how many times?"

"This is the fourth. And there have been five break-ins."

"Maybe she had someone else here the other time."

Tess looks from Amy to Patrick to Amy again, confused. "How do you know there have only been five?"

The carvings. She must not read the newspaper. Of course, Amy doesn't read the paper either. But her parents do. And she's heard things around town. Small-town gossip. Suburbia practically injects the stuff right into the aching, desperate vein of the population. "Every house had the same thing carved into the wall," she tells her. Twice it was a wall. One time a door. Another, a cabinet. With the last break-in the letters had been carved into a cutting board.

"That's right," Patrick laughs, leaning in toward Sadie dramatically. "*Shhhhhhhhh!*" he hisses in her face. Laughing, she swats him away. Amy wants to look at Miles for solidarity, but can't bring herself in this moment to actually need him.

Patrick's right, though. Whoever broke in left the same warning in every house: sʜ! It had been quickly and crudely carved in thick, bulky lettering. Amy's mother found the whole thing incredibly disturbing. Amy was mildly fascinated, because the carving sounded like it would make such a very good movie detail. Only little things were taken from the homes. Arbitrary things. Nothing like a typical robbery.

She doesn't like Patrick suggesting that Eleanor is a thief, though, because being a single mother must be hard enough without people talking about you. Making up stories. Patrick is still giggling and running a hand up Sadie's thigh. She can't tell if he does it because he's actually horny all the time or he just want to embarrass everyone else.

"Barry said he left glass at the foot of the stairs in one of the houses," Miles announces to no one in particular. They all look at him—even Patrick and Sadie.

"What?"

"No shit."

"Where'd he hear that?" asks Amy. There was nothing about broken glass in the paper—her dad would surely have belabored the strangeness of the point if there had been. But she knows the answer even as the question leaves her lips, because Barry's dad is a cop. Miles shifts in her direction—startled that she's speaking to him again.

"Glass?" says Tess. "Like they broke in through a window?"

Miles shakes his head. "A man got up early to make coffee after the break-in, stepped on broken glass going down the stairs—like, someone had left it there on purpose to be stepped on. Needed eight stitches, Barry said."

Amy can't help but wince. She's particularly sensitive about feet.

"The police don't want people talking about it," Miles explains. "Think it will make the public nervous."

"It should," adds Amy. The pointedness of the remark draws more attention than she'd intended. Miles is staring at her again. Amy stands up. His eyes follow her as she goes into the kitchen and grabs Ben's book fair catalogue off the table. When she returns to the hallway she nods in the direction of the stairs. "I'm going to check on the kids."

Miles opens his mouth like he's going to tell her to wait or stay, but before he can do either she makes her exit. Serves him right.

The worn, flattened carpet soft against her sock-clad feet, Amy hurries up the steps. As she reaches the top the music downstairs begins blaring again. The walls are thin and it's way too loud, even up here. She clenches her teeth, sighs, and gently raps her knuckles on Mira's door.

After a moment, Amy presses her ear in close to the door, trying to tell whether the girl is awake or not. She hears the bed creak, then the sound of feet shuffling across the carpet. She takes a step back as the door opens, and when Mira sees that it is Amy come to check on her and not someone more interesting, the girl folds her arms, eyes the catalogue in Amy's hand, and says nothing.

Amy flashes a smile. "How's it going?"

Mira peers out into the hallway, her attention drawn in the direction of the stairs.

"I know," Amy agrees. "The music is too loud. I'm sorry. I keep telling them."

"Why did you invite them here?"

"I didn't. Believe me."

Mira's lips purse at this, as if dismayed that the person supposedly in charge seems to have no authority. Or perhaps Amy is just projecting this onto her. It is difficult to tell. Either way, annoyance prickles at the back of her neck.

"So." Amy tries to get her voice to strike an upbeat chord. It does not. "What have you been up to?"

"Nothing."

Amy looks around the room. A hardcover copy of *Beloved* by Toni Morrison is lying on the bed facedown, to bookmark where she must have left off. "Your Mom said it was okay for you to read that book?" she asks.

Mira shrugs. "I guess."

"It's sort of . . ." Amy tries to find a word that won't offend the preteen but can't. "Mature."

"The library let me borrow it," the girl replies flatly.

Are there age restrictions on taking out books at the library? Amy doesn't know. She's never spent that much time there. Her father's constantly criticizing her for it, telling her to turn off the television and pick up a book. Her father doesn't do a lot of reading, but for some reason he expects Amy to take an interest in it. This wouldn't bother Amy so much except for the way her father talks about movies, like they're a waste of time—garbage fed to the youth en masse.

Amy peers over Mira's head, deeper into the bedroom. "Where's your brother?"

Mira points down the hall, beyond the little boy's own room to the door at the end. Their mother's room. Amy frowns.

"He's been in there the whole time?"

"Pretty much."

"Will your mom mind?"

"No . . . not that she'd notice."

Amy pivots toward Eleanor's room.

"Your friend . , ," continues Mira, regaining the babysitter's attention. "That girl.

"She's not my friend."

"She said I'd look better with bangs."

"She says that to everybody."

Mira takes this at face value, saying nothing. Amy heads down the hall to Eleanor's closed bedroom door. She knocks, but no one answers.

She knocks again.

But still, no sound.

When Amy was about Ben's age her most regular babysitter was a sixteen-year-old girl named Nancy. The first time Amy watched *Nightmare on Elm Street* and saw Nancy Thompson she smiled, because it reminded her of her own Nancy. Nancy the babysitter was something of a math genius—could rattle off numbers and figures like nothing Amy had ever seen, and as young as she was at the time, she could still tell that it was an impressive talent. Nancy was pretty, too, with beautiful green eyes and dark hair and thick glasses. A nerd, but the kind that was so exceptional inside and out that people took notice.

The few times Nancy brought Amy to the mall teenage boys would flock around them, not that Nancy seemed to care. When she was with Amy she was with Amy and was determined to give the awkward, quiet child in her care the benefit of complete and undivided attention. Whenever Amy was sad or worried about something, Nancy could sense it and would come and sit down next to her and talk it through. Amy cried the day Nancy went off to college—Stanford, of course—because she knew she was losing a friend. An ally. Nancy was replaced by Annie, who was always impatient for Amy's parents to return so she could go meet up with her friends. Annie didn't last long. Then came Sadie. Nancy was the good girl. If life were a horror movie, she would have been the star who outwits the killer. Annie, she was the troublemaker. The kind killed off in the first act. As for Sadie, Amy wasn't sure who Sadie would be. She's bold but careful—good at everything but doesn't seem to enjoy most of the areas in which she excels. It's like she's always on the lookout for something, but Amy can't tell what it is.

Gingerly turning the handle, Amy opens the door slowly, only pushing it out about halfway. Enough to peek inside. She's never been in Eleanor's room before and tries not to judge the sea of chaos raging before her. There are clothes scattered across the floor and piled high on the chair in the corner. A number of the dresser drawers are open to different degrees, as if recently ransacked. The bed is made but unevenly so, and the table next to it is home to a collection of loose lipsticks and costume jewelry.

Ben is sitting by the open closet, a big leather-bound book out on the burgundy rug in front of him. He notices her immediately, startled even though Amy had taken such care not to startle him. His muscles go rigid and his eyes fall still. Her little deer. Staring straight into the high beams.

She smiles, wanting to be a Nancy for him. To make him feel safe. "Hey there."

His lips part, then close, then part again. "Do you need help with the thermistit?"

"The what?"

"The thermistit," he says again. "You have to hit it sometimes. Mom said to tell you."

The thermostat. He's talking about the thermostat. Amy resists the deep desire to giggle. "No—not unless it's too chilly up here?"

Ben shakes his head.

"Good," she replies. "What are you looking at?"

"Pictures."

"Pictures?"

Ben nods.

"I can look with you," she says. "If you want."

Ben looks beyond Amy down the hall, his gaze following the echo of the music. A shadow falls across his face.

"What do you say?" she prods, and his attention returns to her. The boy's head bobs up and down like a buoy out at sea.

Amy comes into the room, closing the door behind her as to drown out some of the noise. She finds a place on the floor near the bed, pushing aside a dress and a pile of loose socks, and sits with one ankle folded over the other. She flattens the book catalogue on the carpet and looks at Ben. He's just so sweet. So innocent. She can't help but want to cheer him up—chase the gloom from his tender little eyes. Ben points to a picture in the book, one of a young Eleanor with a pregnant belly and hair curlers. She's laughing. Eyes closed. Skin smooth and pale from the flash of the camera bulb. Shoulders hunched up and just a little forward. She's younger in this image than Amy is now. "Mom," Ben explains, his finger sliding from his mother's neck to her stomach. "M."

"She's beautiful," Amy notes. The boy agrees only by nodding, turning the page. The next photograph shows a screaming little baby in a bassinet—soft red hair and even redder skin. The poor child's face looks like it's about to pop. "I take it that's Mira?"

"She cried a lot."

"I bet."

The photographs progress slowly. There are few more of Mira as a baby, two where she's inconsolable and one where she appears fast asleep. Eleanor is holding her in the latter, her hair pulled back in a loose bun. With the baby tucked safely in her right arm, Eleanor is stroking the infant's cheek with her left hand. And Eleanor looks to be mid laugh. Eyes closed. Shoulders up. She's probably like this in all of them, Amy thinks, though she does not speculate out loud. Not with Ben so busy examining each and every picture the way one would a map. Figuring out where the lines lead. How they connect. Intersect. Divide.

"What happened here?" asks Amy as they continue looking, her hand falling into the book to keep Ben from passing a page. The photograph in the bottom corner has been ripped in half.

"Mom tore Dad out," says Ben, staring down sadly at the photo. His fingers loop around the cord to the mezuzah around his neck. He says nothing else on the subject, and Amy runs a hand through his soft, feathery hair.

"You look at these a lot?" she asks.

Proceeding to the last page, one that bears a picture of Mira and Ben maybe a year or two younger than they are now, the boy nods again.

"Do you remember when this one was taken?" she asks, tapping at the picture.

His expression sours. "This was M's birthday. She wanted this big book series, but we couldn't afford it. Mom got her a journal instead. She was real mad."

"I can see why she'd be upset." Maybe Eleanor had thought that, with a journal, Mira could write her own stories. But when you're a kid, it doesn't matter if your mom has good intentions. "It's disappointing when you want something and you don't get it."

"She knew, though," he tells her. "She knew she wasn't going to get them, but when she opened the journal and saw what it was, she was angry anyway."

"I'm sure she's not angry now."

Ben looks up at her rather seriously. "M is always angry."

"She knows your mom does what she can. You know that too, right?"

Ben's thumb and forefinger rub across the silver edging of his mezuzah. He shrugs.

"Your mom loves you very, very, very, very, *very* much."

"I know."

"Your sister too."

He rolls his eyes, looking just a little bit like Mira "M only loves Mom.

Amy frowns. "That's not true—why would you think that?"

He shrugs.

"Mira loves you," Amy insists, nudging his arm with her elbow. "And I'm pretty fond of you myself."

He looks up at her, eyes bright but reserved. She smooths a stray hair near his face. "You're lucky," she tells him. "A lot of ladies care about you."

"Really?"

"Really," she says. She lifts the catalogue off the floor and holds it out to him. "Want me to help you pick out some good books?"

He eyes the catalogue, then looks back up at her expectantly. "Have you read them?"

"All of them?"

He nods.

Amy laughs. "A few, probably. But I do a lot of babysitting so I know enough about them to—"

The sound of something crashing downstairs leads to a clamor of hollering. Amy's teeth bear down, forcing her to release a breath through her nose. She touches the back of Ben's head with her fingers and tries to smile. "I'm gonna go take care of that," she tells him, handing off the catalogue. "You pick out your favorites, okay?"

Standing up, Amy has to shake the pins and needles loose from her left calf as she heads back into the hallway. Mira's door is closed again. Apparently the sound hasn't disturbed her, or if it has, she doesn't want to get involved. Rushing down the stairs, Amy enters the living room to find Patrick and Sadie on the floor, an end table knocked on its side. They're both laughing mercilessly, and Miles, now on his feet, is yelling at them to cut it out. Tess is busy picking at a crust of pizza, the fingers from her other hand close to her mouth as she watches.

"You need to leave," Amy snaps.

Only Tess looks in her direction. "Betty Crocker!" she laughs. "Want to join the party?"

"You need to leave," Amy says again. "Now."

"They don't have a car," Miles reminds her.

"Then you drive them."

"No, but—"

"Or give them your car. I don't care. They just need to be gone."

"*Come onnn*, Ames," Patrick croons.

"Oh, for fuck's sake!" Amy shouts. The force of her own voice surprises everyone, most of all herself. But she stands her ground. Because the Mazinskis deserve better than this. And because Eleanor would not be scared of Patrick.

Patrick sits up, smirking, and rests a forearm on his knee. "Promise you'll bang my baby bro and we'll go."

Amy lunges at him—*actually* lunges—but Miles catches her before she can drop to the floor and pummel Patrick to a pulp. Tess giggles, covering her mouth with her hand, while Sadie remains calm, unreadable. Patrick's eyes shine with pride as Miles presses his lips close to Amy's ear. "He's not worth it," he whispers.

Patrick raises a hand. "Should we all take that as a maybe?"

Miles looks at him angrily. "Can you shut up?"

"What? This is fun!"

"You know it's not," says Miles.

Sadie places a hand on Patrick's shoulder, close to his neck. "Come on, babe. Let's leave these lovebirds alone."

When he turns to look at her, she closes her eyes and kisses him long and hard.

Tess sighs. Miles's hand remains flat and tense against Amy's back.

Opening her eyes again, Sadie grins and whispers something in Patrick's ear too softly for anyone else to hear. He laughs and she smiles and they stand up slowly, taking their time. Patrick looks back at Amy and Miles, squinting suggestively.

"What?" Amy snaps.

"Nothing." He shrugs, hooking his arm around Sadie's neck. "I didn't say nothing."

Miles hands off his keys and Amy follows them all into the hallway. Miles opens the door and tells his brother to drive carefully. His license was suspended a month ago—too many speeding tickets—but Tess is clearly drunk and Sadie doesn't drive.

Suddenly there's a sound on the stairs and Amy looks up to see Mira standing there, watching them with lowered, critical eyes. It might just be Amy's imagination, but she's almost certain the girl's face shifts into a scowl as her gaze passes over Patrick.

"See you around, peanut," Sadie calls up to her. Amy waits to hear the sound of Miles closing the door behind them before she can bring herself to even look at her boyfriend.

"I'm sorry," he says.

"Right," she mutters. When she looks to the stairs again, Mira is gone.

"Hey," he says, taking her arm. "Really. I'm sorry I brought them here. I didn't think it would—"

"You knew exactly what it would do!" The line of her mouth goes straight and Amy heads back into the living room to tidy up before Eleanor gets home.

"Let me help," offers Miles, but by the time he's done speaking the table is already upright and Amy is back to looking at him. Her arms crossed. Lips puckered slightly. Like she might scream.

"I don't know what Pat said to you, but it doesn't matter what he tells either of us. We can take our time with . . . you know . . ." He shrugs sheepishly.

"You think that's why I'm mad?"

His cheeks color bashfully.

"That's a part of it, yeah, but I'm not some goddamn pushover, Miles. His shit I can take, it's these kids. Do you have any idea what they have been through?"

Amy heard some of it from Eleanor herself, some of it from her own mother, who heard gossip in town. Eleanor and the kids were poor—real poor—living in motels for years until they were able to get an apartment. And Eleanor's boyfriend, the one who had gotten her pregnant in high school, he was as mean as they come. Apparently, he liked to argue with his fists and used to throw around just about everything that wasn't nailed down. Eleanor gave as good as she got, but in the end decided it wasn't worth it. Not for her and not for her kids. She got a restraining order. Moved Mira and Ben and changed their last name to the one she'd grown up with: Mazinski. She got a secretarial position in an accounting office and did the best she could to keep her children fed. Clothed. Safe.

About a year ago, Eleanor's grandmother died and left her every-thing. She sold the woman's modest one-bedroom home, and the money from that, combined with what she'd inherited, was enough to get them a house in Chase Hills. The last thing Mira and Ben needed was the likes of Patrick Murphy coming in and dragging his own particular brand of chaos through their lives. A reminder of what they'd hoped to leave behind.

"They need stability," Amy tells him. "And security. What they don't need is an asshole with a big mouth breaking all their shit."

"He didn't break anything."

"That's not the point!" Amy yells. "Dear God, Miles! I know he's your brother, and I'm not asking you to disown him, but the least you could do is keep him away when I'm working! When I'm responsible for some-one's kids!"

"Amy , , "

His eyes are pleading with her, begging for forgiveness, but all she sees is that look on Ben's face right before he went upstairs. The way he scurried after Mira. Not just uncomfortable, but scared. "Ms. Maz-inski trusts me," she says, her expression stiff. She waits for Miles to say something—to continue defending his brother or maybe apologize for the way he stood by and let Patrick take over. Only he does neither, and this—this, above all the rest—is what disappoints her most.

"I think maybe you should go too," she says at last.

"What?"

"I think you should just leave. Let me do my job here," she explains. She doesn't want him to go—she wants just the opposite, really—but she's too angry to look at him right now.

"They took my car," he reminds her.

Amy crosses the room to her backpack, pulls the zipper on the front pouch, and digs out her keys. She holds them up to him. "Here."

"How will you get home?"

"I can call my mom," she replies. "She'll pick me up."

"Amy, I'm . . . can we just . . ."

Rising to her feet, she walks over to him and puts the keys in his hands. Cradling his fingers in her own for just a second, she slowly draws away again. "Please," she says. "We can talk about it tomorrow."

His brow furrowed, Miles leans in to kiss her on the cheek, but Amy pivots away. She does not watch him walk to the front hall. Does not look at him as he waits for her to change his mind. And it is only after he's closed the door and she's gone and locked it behind him that Amy leans her back against the door. Hands shaking. Vision blurring.

Her stomach knots and loosens and knots again.

And just as everything around her goes dark and dim and shaky, she begins to cry.

The dough was soft and sweet and Amy could taste the crunch of sugar in it as she chewed. Sadie had insisted on adding an extra quarter teaspoon of vanilla—said they tasted better that way. Amy scraped the bowl with the edge of a wooden spoon and took another bite of cookie dough—the last bite, as the cookies were now safely baking. Sadie offered to wash the bowl out while Amy put everything else away, and when they were done Sadie peeked inside the oven, dimples showing as she tossed a smile over her shoulder. "Is there any smell in the world better than fresh cookies?"

Personally, Amy liked the smell of gasoline at the gas station, but she could tell that wasn't an answer she was supposed to give. At least her stomachache had gone away. For now. Sometimes it felt like her anxiety came and went in waves, sweeping her out to sea only to throw her back into the sand. Breathless but safe.

"These will be done soon," continued Sadie, straightening up and placing her hands on her hips. She was skinny enough that even a plain sweater looked fashionable and sophisticated draped across her frame. Her legs were long, making her taller than Amy's mother but shorter than her father and cousins. And to top it all off, Sadie's cheekbones gave her whole face a very fancy quality, while her expressions remained consistently friendly. Approachable.

Amy wished she could be pretty like this girl: capable and confident, with chocolate chips in her backpack. Only, Amy knew her own face was too boring, her body too frumpy. She'd been skinny as a rail in elementary school, but her body was changing. Expanding in places that made other kids laugh at her. Twice last year she'd been marked absent by Mrs. Stein for attendance simply because her teacher had overlooked her. What was it like to be pretty like Sadie? What kind of confidence did the certainty of that beauty bring her? "We can start going over your homework while they cool," suggested Sadie.

Startled, Amy stared, then frowned. "Just the math," she half said, half asked—fishing for confirmation. Her parents never checked her homework in other subjects. Besides, she'd finished those assignments after she'd gotten home from school.

Sadie nodded. Those dimples. "Just the math," she agreed. "Then we can do whatever we want. Your mom said you like movies?"

Amy thought about the movies Charlie and Donnie would show her and almost cackled the way her cousins did when they thought something was dumb. Instead, she bit down on the inside of her lip and nodded. "Do you like doing this?" she asked, eager to change the subject. And curious too. Amy couldn't figure out why someone as cool as Sadie would want to spend time with some kid.

"Doing what, peanut?"

"Watching boys and girls like me."

Sadie cocked her head to the side. "I don't think I've ever met a girl like you before."

Clearly, Sadie had meant it as a compliment, but Amy, unable to see herself as deserving, assumed it meant there was something wrong with her—something that made her less fun or interesting than the other children Sadie babysat.

"I enjoy making cookies, doing homework," Sadie continued. "Always have. If I can share that with someone and make a little money in the process, what's not to like?"

"Kids," Amy blurted out.

Sadie laughed. "Kids aren't scary. Believe me. In fact, they're exciting. Adults can be predictable, but kids? You never know what a kid is going to do or say. As a kid, you're just free to be yourself. You don't have to worry about anything else." She glanced up to check the time above the stove. "Well, that should do it! Where do your parents keep the pot-holders?"

Amy directed her sitter to the appropriate cabinet, where a pair of dark red, partially burned oven mitts were retrieved. Sadie took the cookies out and set them on the stovetop to cool.

"Congratulations," she said as Amy came to examine the fruits of their labor. "You, peanut, just made your very own batch of chocolate chip cookies."

CHAPTER ELEVEN

BEN

"Who is it?"

"Who do you think?"

"I don't know."

"Her boyfriend. Obviously."

"Amy doesn't have a boyfriend."

"Yes, she does. He was here last time."

"That wasn't her boyfriend."

"Yes," M sighs, stretching her painted toes out across the carpet. "It was."

Ben flashes a troubled look at the front hall, and while he can't see who Amy's talking to at the door, he can hear that she's laughing. "That wasn't her boyfriend," he says again. Before his sister can argue, Ben slips off the couch and heads for the hallway to get a better look.

"You will like them," Amy is insisting. Ben can only see her back, but he knows she's smiling. Amy always sounds different when she's smiling. Sunnier. Warmer. "I *swear.*"

"That's what you said last time," says the boy at the door, the same one who'd shown up the last time Amy was over. He's tall, but boring looking—much too boring to be Amy's boyfriend. Dark hair. Faded jeans. Absolutely no *class*, as Mom would say. She says you can tell the difference between a man and a boy trying to be a man by seeing if he has any *class*. "And *Halloween*?" the boy continues. "How can you even watch that? You're a babysitter."

Amy shrugs. "It's not like it's based on a true story."

"Are horror movies ever based on true stories?"

"Yeah! I mean, very loosely, but yeah. *Texas Chainsaw* . . . *The Exorcist* . . . *Amityville Horror* . . . but seriously—just give *Halloween* a shot. It's all fake anyway. They shot this thing on a super-low budget. They even had to re-use all the same leaves to make it look like fall everywhere. Isn't that funny? Come on. If you get scared, I'll let you put your arm around me."

Ben doesn't like how close they're standing. Too close. Like she might fall into him. He doesn't know what they're talking about, but he's mad that the boy is disagreeing with Amy. Because Amy seems like the type of person who always knows what she's talking about. Slowly Ben's feet shuffle forward without his consent. His knees shake. By the time he manages to regain control of his feet he's standing only five feet away from them. Amy's back is still turned, but the boy sees Ben, and Ben's ready for him to be annoyed. He's seen that look a thousand times whenever guys try to talk to Mom at the mall or the park. Only this boy doesn't appear angry that Ben is here. He almost looks friendly. Guys at the mall and the park have tried this approach too. Being nice to the kids. Ben knows better than to trust it. Because M has warned him that they are only ever nice because they want Mom to like them.

"What?" asks Amy, spinning around. Her gentle eyes flicker at the sight of him and Ben's heart skips just a little bit fast. "Hey," she says. "Remember Miles?"

"You've got yourself a pretty awesome sitter here, Ben," says this supposed Miles, hands in his pockets like a hoodlum. Mom always says hoodlums are no good. Worse than regular boys. Because hoodlums are trouble.

Outside there's a loud bang. Ben jumps.

Amy tips forward out the doorway. "Who's in your car?"

The hoodlum pulls her back into the house, and Ben wants to walk right up and kick him in the shin for grabbing at her like that. "Listen," stammers Miles. "About that . . ."

"What?"

"Just . . . hear me out. Please don't get mad, okay?"

Amy already looks plenty mad. "Why would I get mad?"

Miles won't—or can't—say. Ben tries to make his face look stern—the way M's always does when they meet one of Mom's boyfriends—but he's not sure he's doing it right. Maybe he's squinting too much. Or maybe he's got his mouth too twisted around. Last time he tried to make this face they were at a restaurant with one of the guys who wanted to convince Mom he liked kids—invited them all out to dinner. M was not pleased, but Mom has told them again and again never to turn down free food, and so M did her best not to look too mad. Ben didn't like the guy, though. A real hoodlum. He didn't know how Mom couldn't see it. He laughed at his own jokes, but not hers, and even though he'd told her to bring her kids he ignored the both of them all night long. When Ben tried to make M's stern face at the man, Mom saw and asked if he had to go to the bathroom.

"Why would I get mad?" Amy repeats.

Before Miles can muster up an answer, two strangers come stumbling in, a boy and a girl. They look like the sort of friends Mom had back when Mom had friends. At least they're how M always describes her friends as looking—loose, free limbs and careless smiles. Ben doesn't really remember them much. When he pictures them in his head, he just pictures a dozen Aunt Pattys.

That's all right, though. He doesn't need to remember them all.

Because M has always done the remembering for the both of them.

The strangers head for the living room, and suddenly Ben's chest constricts. He should warn M that they're here, but he feels trapped in the hall. His feet, which have stopped listening to him again, remain glued to the floor. Another girl comes in and moves past him as if he's not even there. Amy is saying things now—harsh things to Miles in a sort of loud whisper. Now he's sure Amy is doing the stern look right, her gaze sharp and face very, very serious. He's never seen Amy mad before, but she kind of looks the way Mom looks whenever she's annoyed. It doesn't scare him. In fact, it's a little comforting—

The floorboards creak and Ben realizes M has come up next to him. She's watching Amy and Miles, her eyes keen and careful. She seems to be just about as skeptical as he is about this Miles person. Ben hopes she'll say something mean to him—something to startle him. M is good at that.

Only, before she can, Amy sees her standing there and goes rigid.

"Your friends are unappealing," says M in her grown-up talk voice. Whenever she wants to sound older, she uses this voice, throwing around big words and speaking lower than she normally does. She almost sounds a little like Mom when she does it. Almost. Only she's scratching at the inside of her wrist, and Ben knows it means she's uncomfortable. He's disappointed. Because he doesn't think she's included Miles in her observation.

"They are not my friends," Amy replies, looking meanly at Miles. A grin flutters between Ben's lips. He tries to force it into a frown just to keep it from flying off his face.

He waits for M to say something else—something about Miles and his ugly jeans. Only she's leaving now—on her way upstairs. And even though Ben would prefer to spend more time with Amy, he doesn't like the thought of his sister leaving him all alone with the boy and the girls and Miles, who may or may not be Amy's boyfriend.

He sprints, trailing fast after M up the stairs. He assumes she'd be going to her own room, but by the time he reaches the top of the stairs he sees her disappearing into Mom's room. He waits to see if she's going to invite him to join her, and when she doesn't Ben goes and stands in the doorway. Waiting.

M, having fallen forward on the bed, is flipping lazily through a magazine. Even with her back to him, though, she can sense her brother's presence. It sends a rigidness down her spine. "Go away," she warns him, but she must be waiting to hear his feet shuffling against the carpet, because when he doesn't move, she flips over and sits up. The magazine is still lying open on the comforter. "What do you want?" She sighs, sliding off the bed. She pulls her hair back as she comes to the door, like she's going to put it up in a ponytail. Only it's too short and when she lets go the hair falls back around her face.

Ben nods in the direction of the magazine. "I thought you didn't like those."

"I don't, but the library's closed," she remarks distastefully. "So, unless you've changed your mind and want me to do your nails . . ."

Ben shakes his head, and the boredom, temporarily suspended, re- turns to his sister's expression. She still has three library books in her room. She could be in there if she wanted to be, only he thinks she is just a little bit afraid of her new room. M would never admit it, but he can tell.

M doesn't wait for him to leave. Instead, she spins around and re- turns to the bed. Only Ben doesn't go to his room like she wants. He walks through the threshold of the doorway and sits on the corner of the bed by his sister's feet. M ignores him, knowing that talking to him— even if it's just to tell him to get lost—will only make him hang around longer. There's laughing coming from downstairs and M visibly shud- ders. "I hate her friends," she grumbles, pulling the magazine back in front of her.

"Amy said they're not her friends."

"Whoever they are, they're boring."

"They're loud."

"Same thing," says M, glancing back at him over her shoulder. "You're just not big enough to understand it."

"Aunt Patty's loud."

"Yeah, but Aunt Patty's original. It's okay, as long as you're original."

Ben slides a finger across a fraying thread on Mom's comforter, flattening it with his thumb. He doesn't think there's really any difference at all between them and Aunt Patty.

"Don't you have homework?" asks M, returning to her magazine. Mom's magazine. Ben isn't entirely sure she's actually reading it. In fact, he's sure she's not. Because her eyes move fast from side to side to side when she's reading something, and right now she's staring hard at the very center where the pages meet.

"No."

"Oh, to be young," she says and sighs. It's something she's started saying a lot lately, even though she's not old enough herself to be considered *not* young. M's an old soul. That's what Mom says. Ben doesn't really know how one becomes an old soul, but Mom always seems pretty sure of herself when she says it. He wonders if M knows this about herself, or if it's a secret Mom doesn't want him to share. She always whispers when she says it, as if M might hear and dare to disagree.

"In a few years you'll start to get homework on the weekends," she tells him. "Then you'll see."

"I don't mind."

"Yeah, you wouldn't mind, would you?"

He presses down hard on the loose thread, watching his thumb slowly turn redder and redder. Then he removes his finger altogether and folds one hand over the other. "Do you have homework?" he asks.

She continues to not read the magazine. He doesn't want to be alone, and so he stays, comforted by his sister's presence. Even if she doesn't want him here. He'd rather be her unwanted shadow than stuck all by himself.

He looks down at the comforter, then back at M. "Why do you think she likes him?"

"Who?"

"Miles."

M glances over her shoulder. "Maybe he's a good kisser."

M's attention quickly returns to the magazine, but Ben's cheeks color—and through her big-sister Spidey-sense she feels it, because she sighs and sits up and slides her legs around so that she's facing her little brother. "Don't sweat it," she tells him. He turns his head away, but M redirects it with a finger under his chin. Just like Mom always does. "She's too old for you, anyway."

Ben's brow tightens and he must look mad because M starts to laugh. She never laughs at him unless she's making fun of him, but she doesn't seem to be doing that now. She almost feels like Mom for a moment, loving and kind and certain beyond all certainty. But it is only for a moment, because as her hand drops from his chin the affection fresh in her eyes fizzles out.

"He's probably a bad kisser," she decides. "Amy's just the kind of girl who can't tell the difference between a good kisser and a bad one."

Ben knows his sister doesn't know anything about kissing. Or Amy. Or any of it. But something about that look she gave him just before she became herself again is still lingering with him. He smiles. M smiles back. And ruffles his hair. And laughs again. M's never nice, but when she is, she makes him feel like the most popular boy in the world. She makes him feel loved and safe and seen. Like he belongs somewhere with someone. Part of a family.

Suddenly the phone rings, ripping the quiet around them straight down the seam. Ben's eyes flicker. "It's Mom!" he cries, knowing she wouldn't call but hoping anyway, as if saying it will make it true. It rings again and he leaps across the bed, even as M reaches out and yells his name. Only he doesn't listen. She grabs his foot, but he wriggles free, falling onto the floor next to the nightstand.

He scrambles up. Lifts the receiver to his ear.

"No!" M hisses. "Don't!"

"Hello?" says Ben. "Mom?"

Through the phone he hears someone breathing—a steady stream of long breaths.

"Mom?" he says again.

It has to be her—it just has to be—but before she can speak M pulls the phone from his hands and shoves it back down on the console. She whips around at him, eyes raging. Ben stumbles back into the bed, startled.

"What are you doing?" M barks, gripping Ben tightly by the shoulders, whispering and shouting at the same time, like she's afraid that whoever had called might still be listening. A rush of color spreads across her cheeks. Red. Like her blood is boiling out. He shakes. "You're not supposed to answer the phone!"

"I thought it was Mom."

"It wasn't Mom!"

"But how do you—"

"It wasn't Mom," she snaps. "And if it was, Amy would have gotten it and told us. But it wasn't her. And you shouldn't be talking to strangers."

Ben doesn't understand why she's so angry. M's mean all the time, sure, but she's acting like he's hurt her on purpose. He hasn't. Really. He just wants to talk to Mom. She's been gone for so long. He doesn't know why his sister's eyes are still so hard, but he doesn't like it.

"There are three rules," she reminds him. "Don't answer the phone. Don't answer the door. And don't talk to strangers. You just violated numbers one *and* three."

"I thought it was . . ." he begins, slowly falling silent. The word *Mom* drying up in his mouth. He looks at the floor and it is only as M lets go of him that he realizes just how deeply her fingers had been biting into his skin. She leans back, away from him, and starts scratching the inside of her wrist, nails dragging across the skin so sharply he's worried they'll draw blood. "Who was it, then?" he asks quietly.

She doesn't say anything. Just keeps scratching.

"Who was it?"

"No one."

"But who was it?"

"The ghost!"

"You said there is no gh—"

"I lied," she tells him. Her arms fall to her sides. "There is one and he's mean, and if you answer the phone, he'll reach out from it and pull you in and eat you up."

Ben studies her face, not wanting her to be right, but finding himself afraid anyway. The sensation creeps and crawls through his head like spiders in his brain. It tickles. Hurts. And terrifies him. He swallows hard. "How do I know you're not lying now?"

"If you don't believe me, then go ahead," she offers. "Pick up the phone."

Carefully the boy's eyes shift, bringing the phone into focus. His fingers tremble, but otherwise his hands remain exactly where they are. He won't try it—and M knows he won't. Their house is haunted, and while he wants to believe the ghost is good, he doesn't really know for sure. And so, he just stands there as M shrugs and turns, abandoning the magazine. He doesn't see her leave, but after a beat he hears her door at the other end of the hall slam shut.

A few minutes pass. Mom's boom box starts up again downstairs. Ben usually finds it comforting, but he doesn't now. Because he's afraid it will anger the ghost. And he does not want him to be angry.

He lingers in Mom's empty room, waiting to see what the ghost will do next.

Hoping M isn't right.

But knowing, like he always knows, that she is.

CHAPTER TWELVE

AMY

FRIDAY, OCTOBER 15, 1993
9:12 P.M. (2 HOURS AND 48 MINUTES BEFORE MIDNIGHT)

Bob has just gone to get beer and Amy knows he won't be back. It doesn't matter how many times she's seen this movie, the music is so good and the tension is so carefully drawn out. Every time she rents it, she feels like she's watching it for the first time. That's the mark of a good film right there, or so she's always telling Miles.

He hasn't called since he left, for which she is relieved and a little disappointed. Not that she wants to be temperamental—the one who kicks him out and then pouts when he doesn't call her. It's just been a long day and an even longer night. She hates Patrick and is angry with Miles and all she wants to do is watch this guy get a knife right through the chest.

It's not exactly the kill itself she's waiting for. The first time she ever saw *Halloween* she was about eleven. Her cousins, Charlie and Donnie—a high school sophomore and a high school junior at the time— were babysitting while all their parents went out to dinner. This was after Annie but before Sadie. Charlie and Donnie had secretly rented the movie from the video store after their mom warned them against bringing anything scary over to the house. They'd both seen the movie before, but it was all new to Amy. While they jumped and cheered at the good kills and threw popcorn at the television whenever they got bored, Amy was fascinated by the tiny things—the little moments in between the stabbing and running and screaming.

And this moment coming up—it is the best. Her favorite movie moment of all time. It's just after Michael Myers stabs poor Bob with the knife, using it to tack him up on the wall. The kitchen's all dark except for some loose light reflecting off the refrigerator and the knife's handle. Michael is standing there in his mask all still and patient, and he just *tilts* his head ever so slightly. Like there's something in this death he's trying to find. Amy considers this to be creepier than any of the actual kills or big scares. Because it is so human. And it is so subtle. And maybe, in its own perverted way, it's just a tiny bit beautiful.

The only other shot that even compares is that final look Anthony Perkins gives the camera in *Psycho*, or maybe the blood pouring through the elevator doors in *The Shining*. Just the right implementation of craft and chaos.

Surely Miles wouldn't like any of this. It's all too blunt, too direct for him. He prefers quieter movies, the kinds that win awards and are hailed by critics as revelations. Amy has seen enough of them, and enjoys them, and respects them, but nothing for her could ever take the place of horror. It's a uniquely visceral genre, which is completely thrilling to a girl who always does her homework on time and is home when she says she's going to be home and who never drinks or smokes or does anything terribly shocking. But she has her creature features and her slasher flicks. She knows all the classic famous last words and the most creative ways some hopeless teenager can meet a grisly end.

As Michael kills Bob, Amy leans forward on the couch, squeezing a pillow to her stomach. She waits, eyes wide, for that ever-so-subtle tilt.

There!

Right there!

She falls back into her seat, satisfied with the quality of the film-making. In the quiet subtleties of Michael Myers. In many of Miles's favorite films the characters give these grand, moving speeches just before they die. In horror movies the deaths aren't like that—someone's last line can be arbitrary. A throwaway line. And isn't that closer to life? People don't always know when they're going to die, so they can't possibly imagine their last words are going to be their last words.

It's easy to criticize the teenagers in *Halloween*, shouting from the comfort of your living room for them to turn around or stop having sex and pay attention. How are they supposed to know there's a killer on the loose? How are they supposed to believe that they are next? If people in real life were as all-knowing as they want characters in these movies to be, then there would be far fewer murders in the world. That's for sure.

As the film continues, Amy spins her ring, twisting it round and sliding it back and forth aimlessly. The Mazinski kids have been quiet for a while. She hasn't heard from either one of them since she went up there and found Ben in his mother's room.

Scooping the remote off the seat beside her, Amy presses pause and the screen comes to a trembling stop just as Michael Myers, disguised in the dead boy's sheet and glasses, stands in a doorway. Amy's gaze lingers on this perhaps a moment longer than she'd intended. Then she rises to her feet, stretches out her arms, and wanders behind the couch to the window. Peeking out the beige-brown blinds, she spots the tiniest sliver of a moon hanging in the sky. As if someone had come and cut out the night, exposing the white, bruised underbelly of the universe. There are few things she knows to be as beautifully, haunt-ingly quiet as a night sky.

Glancing over her shoulder, she checks the time on the VCR. Nearly nine thirty. The sun went down a little after six and it's gotten almost frigid out since. She can tell from the chill pulsing off the window and against her cheek.

Supposedly there's going to be close to a full moon for Halloween this year, which seems fitting. Halloween is also going to be on a Sunday, which means there won't be any parties that night. They'll all be on Saturday instead, when people won't have to work the next day. No parties means no sitting, so she'll actually have Halloween itself free.

Pulling away from the window, Amy trails her fingers across the back of the couch. With her free hand she slides that ring back and forth on her figure.

Miles still hasn't called. He knows the Mazinskis' number, and unlike most specimens his age, he's a big fan of talking things out. He prefers to discuss their problems. Encourages it even. Amy suspects it's because his mom is a shrink, but Miles denies it. Says everyone talks this way, but Amy knows from watching her own parents that this simply isn't true.

Maybe she should check on the kids. Just to make sure. Amy goes out of the living room and through the front hall, tiptoeing about halfway up the steps, and listens carefully for signs of trouble or distress. She'd thought Ben would have come back down by now, but he hasn't.

She stays there on the stairs, perfectly still, for about a minute before giving up and going back down again. Checking the time, she moves into the kitchen and lifts the phone off its cradle on the wall and punches in her home number. She'd held off making the call, in case Miles came back, but he hasn't—and even if he did, she's not sure she'd want him to stay.

The phone only rings twice, because her mother hates the sound of it and keeps complaining that they can't adjust the volume. "Hello?" comes her terse, tight voice. She sounds a little sleepy, and it's likely she'd just been dozing on the couch in front of the television.

"Hey, it's me."

"Did the car break down again?" she asks, her voice softening instantly. Amy only ever calls like this if her car won't start.

"No, Ms. Mazinski isn't back yet," Amy replies.

"Is Amy on her way home?" she hears her father yell to her mother from what is probably the kitchen.

"Not yet!" Amy's mom yells back. "She's still waiting on the mother."

Amy hears her father grumble something she can't quite hear, ending with "that woman stays out far too late."

The Bakers stay out just as late. The Millers too. What her father means is that Ms. Mazinski stays out too late for an unmarried woman. And this makes Amy bristle just a little.

Amy twists the phone cord round her finger one, two, three times. "I need a favor."

"Everything all right?" her mom asks her.

"Yeah, I just . . . I was wondering if you could pick me up later?"

"So the car isn't working?"

"No, it's just . . . Miles had to borrow it and he won't be back in time to get me," she explains, hoping that her father isn't listening too closely to the exchange. Her father won't approve of her lending out the car, especially to a teenage boy. "They are all terrible drivers," he says, on a regular basis, whenever they're on the highway. "I should know, I was one of them!"

Her mom's reaction is, fortunately, more merciful. "Of course, sweetie. What time?"

Amy lets the cord loosen around her finger. This is what she loves most about her mother, the way she doesn't ask intrusive questions. She just tackles the problem directly in front of her, whatever that problem might be.

"Not sure, but it might be close to midnight. Or later. I'm really sorry."

"Hey, don't worry about it," she replies, lowering her voice so that Amy's father—who's likely just left earshot—won't hear. "I'm a little buzzed anyway, so it will give me a chance to sober up." She whispers this like some deep, dark secret, and Amy tries not to laugh. "Buzzed" for her mother is a third of a glass of pinot grigio mixed with soda.

"I will call when Ms. Mazinski gets back, is that all right?"

"Yeah, yeah, I will keep the cordless nearby. Wouldn't want to wake your father at that hour."

"Thanks."

"Miles left, did he?" her mother asks, which catches her a little off guard. Because she'd expected this would be the end of the conversation.

Amy hesitates. "Um, yeah. He had to help his brother with something."

"I don't like you over there alone," she says tenderly. It comes from a place of love, Amy knows this, but sometimes she prefers her father's sharpness to her mother's overprotective lectures, because her concerned comments *always* turn into lectures.

"I'm not alone," she reminds her. "The kids are upstairs."

"You know what I mean."

Amy lists in her head all the movies in which she's heard this conversation take place. Too many to count. "I'm supposed to be the paranoid one who's seen too many movies, remember?"

It's a joke her mother would usually find funny, only she doesn't laugh.

"Paranoid has got nothing to do with it," she sighs. "With everything that's been going on around here. You know whoever's breaking into those houses took Mrs. Johnson's earrings. And the Harringtons—their TV remote is missing. A remote of all things! Stolen in the middle of the night. While they were home. In their beds. It's scary stuff."

Amy wants to argue that Leatherface is scary, but doesn't. Her mother is obviously in no mood to hear it. She says nothing about the broken glass, certain her mother doesn't know about it. "The Johnsons and the Harringtons can afford it," Amy tells her. "No one is going to come and take Ms. Mazinski's old remote. It barely works as it is." She feels bad saying this, like she's betraying Eleanor, but it's all she can think of to appease her mother.

"That's not the point."

"All the doors are locked. I know where Ms. Mazinski keeps her baseball bat. Don't worry."

She hates that phrase. *Don't worry.* If she had a dime every time someone in a horror movie said *Don't worry* . . .

"I just love you. You know that."

"I know. I love you too."

"Look after yourself."

"I will. See you in a bit," Amy says quickly, if only to put a stop to any further discussion on the matter. "Bye."

She hangs up before her mother has a chance to say more, and rolling on her heels, Amy falls with her back against the bathroom door. Overprotective parents are a good thing, right? They'd be shitty parents if they weren't like this, worrying about their little girl, wanting to make sure she's safe.

Because she still is their little girl. When has she ever done anything to suggest otherwise? Maybe applying to UCLA. That wasn't something a child would do. Perhaps it might be seen as childish, secretly trying to leave the east coast, but her intentions are sound. She wants to study film, and Los Angeles is the place to do it.

Twisting in her gut is the knowledge that, little girl or not, she has seen this movie before—the one in which no one expects a break-in until suddenly there is one. *When a Stranger Calls, Torso*—Italian horror in general is brutal enough to warrant a little care and consideration. Only, if she believes all this, then her father is right, scary movies have rotted her brain, and she refuses to believe her father is right about anything.

Rubbing her face, Amy returns to the living-room window and presses her fingers to the glass. It is cool and smooth and perfect in that smoothness. A shadow shifts behind her forefinger and as she pulls her hand from the window, she realizes it is not a shadow, but a figure. A person. Emerging from the house across the street. She assumes he'll veer left toward the driveway, but instead the man stops at the edge of the property and looks both ways and crosses the street toward the Mazinski house. Amy squints. Leans in. She recognizes the tweed blazer—beige and brown and somehow wrinkled—even though the man's face remains wrapped in the shadows. As he comes up the Mazinski walkway, Amy goes into the front hall and untwists the lock and pulls open the door.

"Mr. Darren?" she says, though it is more of a question than a greeting. Or perhaps the words are a muddle somewhere in between. Mr. Darren—much older than Amy's father but younger than her grandfather—squints ever so slightly. As if he doesn't quite trust the prescription for his glasses. Only he's not wearing glasses.

"Amy." He says her name with much more certainty than she had said his. Nonetheless, the way he blinks blankly suggests he is just as surprised to see her as she is to see him.

Mr. Darren—Professor Darren, technically—comes to the high school every year to give a talk to the seniors about college applications and what schools are looking for. He even reads admission essays for anyone desiring to go that extra mile, which was precisely what Amy had done.

The professor looks down at the envelope between his hands, then back up to Amy. "I know I have the right house," he says, showing her the envelope. It looks like a bill addressed to Eleanor. "This got dropped in my mailbox by mistake. Would have returned it earlier, but I only just got to going through the mail."

"Ms. Mazinski is out," Amy tells him, taking the bill. Immediately she considers that admitting to Eleanor's absence is not something she should be doing in the presence of strangers, but Mr. Darren isn't a stranger. He's a well-meaning old man. The Dr. Loomis type. If life were a movie, Donald Pleasence would play him.

Besides, Mr. Darren had given Amy a lot of good feedback on the paper she'd submitted to him, *The Auteur and the Genre Film: The Shaping of an Audience*. She revised with all his notes in mind, paring her paragraphs down in order to stay on point and strengthening the ties between this type of filmmaking and her own interest in cinema. He'd seemed to like her topic, though, which her English teacher had said was the important thing. The topic was what would set her apart from other applicants.

"My niece sings your praises," he says with a smile, one that deepens a series of wrinkles around his eyes.

"Your niece?"

"Tiffany," he continues. "She says you're just great with the girls."

"Oh, Mrs. Dumont! Yes! Oh, that's very sweet of her."

"Hope these two aren't giving you too much trouble," he says with a chuckle.

"Not at all," Amy assures him. "They're very low maintenance."

"Now that doesn't surprise me," he replies, slipping his hands into the pockets of his brown slacks. The way he's standing makes him seem younger somehow—or at least like those people who, no matter how old they get, never seem to stop being their former selves. "You know, when they first moved in, I didn't even know there were kids. Imagine that? I love Tiffany's girls, of course, but you can hear those two coming a mile away."

Amy smiles. He's not wrong.

"Anyway, I'm sure you're eager to get back to your evening," he says, stepping away from the doorway.

"I will make sure Ms. Mazinski gets this."

"Great, great."

"Have a good night."

"You too, darlin'."

He smiles, which again shifts the wrinkles around his eyes. As he makes his way back across the street, Amy closes the door and brings the bill into the kitchen, leaving it near the rest of the mail at the edge of the counter.

Returning to the living room, she takes a seat on the couch. She doesn't press play on the remote, though, not right away.

Instead, she listens again for the kids. Trying to determine if they're awake. Mira prefers to be alone and she respects this, but Ben might want company. Maybe he'd like to come back downstairs but is worried she won't want him around. Frowning, she considers the way he looked at her when she told him how much they all care about him. He almost seemed relieved. Like he was worried she might have said something else—something cruel.

Chewing on her lower lip, Amy squeezes her ring and considers going up to see him again when a bang on the front door sends a shock through her bones. She hadn't even realized how still she'd been sitting until she jumps, at least an inch off the couch, and her body whips around toward the door.

There's silence, then the knocking resumes, this time more patiently. Mr. Darren. He must have forgotten to say something.

Amy hurries into the front hall just as the kids arrive on the landing to see what all the fuss is about, but as Amy swings the door open, she realizes very quickly that it is not Mr. Darren returning, or even Miles having come to work things out.

The man standing in the doorway is someone she's never seen before, with days-old scruff and brown-blond hair long enough to be styled just a little, only it's not styled at all. It's loose and slick with sweat. His eyes are brown like dark amber, and as they register the children arriving at the stairs, they offer up a wink. Then his attention returns to Amy, those eyes sinisterly congenial.

Had she listened to anything her mom had said on the phone? Any of it at all?

Don't worry, her brain hums to itself. *Don't worry*. Only, how many teenagers have had their throats slit onscreen after saying something as blatantly counterintuitive as *Don't worry*?

"Can I help you?" Amy asks, because it seems to be the thing to ask—and, if she were anywhere else, she would have done that already.

The man's eyebrows stretch up as he cocks his head to the side. "I don't know. Can you?"

A smile spreads across his face, one gritty with a sort of confidence Amy considers to be rather threatening.

"I'm here for my kids," he tells her, and it is in this moment—this very moment—that she realizes why she's finding it so hard to speak, because she should have figured it out already. And maybe she did. Maybe she understood the second she saw him there on the front porch and that was what had frightened her.

Amy's mouth opens, then closes.

Her brain begins swearing at her. Asshole. Idiot. Lazy bitch. Opening a door without checking the window? Giving some stranger in the middle of the night an opportunity to present himself? Movies have taught her better than this. *The Hitcher*, *Psycho*, and *Halloween*, even, had taught her not to fall into this trap.

That old, familiar stir of instability starts itching inside of her.

The shaking.

The stammering.

The weak knees.

Every panic attack cue comes tumbling in simultaneously. Sensory overload. She can smell her nerve ends frying. She prays she doesn't puke—or black out. One time, at the mall, she actually did black out. And that attack hadn't even been triggered by anything. She was just there with her mom to get socks.

She can imagine herself blacking out now. Crumpling to the floor like paper. Hitting her head. Bleeding out while this man just waltzes right in—no fight, no nothing. Amy knows her body is reacting too strongly to the situation, and yet her brain does not seem to be responding strongly enough.

She needs to get it together, but the more she panics the more she blinks and the spottier everything looks. Feels. Even her thoughts are incomplete, like a puzzle with missing pieces. She knows where they go, what they do, but she can't bring herself to find them. "I—I'm afraid you have the wrong house," she stammers at last, even though they both know he has the right house—or at least the house he intends to be at, never mind if it's actually right for him to be here.

"No," he replies evenly, leaning forward—or maybe just standing in a way that gives him the appearance of leaning forward. Tall in presence as well as in stature. He really does remind her of the guy in *The Hitcher*. What's his name? She knows it—she does—but it's one of those missing puzzle pieces. The name has gone and slipped right out of her head. He shifts his weight and this time she's certain he's moved in a little bit closer. "I don't," he assures her.

"I'm sorry, but I can't help you," she replies hastily, already closing the door before the sentence is through. He shoves a boot in as a stopper and she presses anyway—like the weight of the door might be enough to push him out. It isn't. He forces the door.

Amy takes a step back—not intentionally, just to put some distance between them. Immediately she sees the error in this, because now there is suddenly this gaping hole in the hallway. An open wound of possibility. Mira's still frozen where she stands on the landing, but Ben scurries down the steps to Amy, seeking shelter at her side. In truth, his little body beside hers is the only thing keeping her propped up; she'd likely tumble over otherwise.

There's still that wide-open space in front of the door for the man to enter. And he does just that, stepping inside like he's lived here all along. Casual and certain and entitled in the way only a man who isn't very good at being a man can be. He waves his hand at Ben. "Hey, kiddo."

The line of Amy's mouth tightens. "Ms. Mazinski is upstairs and if she—"

"Ellie ain't here." He laughs, revealing a set of pretty but slightly crooked teeth. "B doesn't answer the phone when she's here," he says, his eyes shifting back again to the boy. "Do you, B?"

Ben clings to Amy's wrist. When the babysitter's eyes dart back to the stairs, Mira is no longer there. Amy takes another step back, just to move Ben a little farther away from his father.

"I want to see my kids," he continues, closing the door behind him. This one, simple act sends a terrible pull through Amy's insides like a thread unraveling. She's suddenly very aware of how alone the four of them are in this house.

A buzzing in her head grows louder.

The Hitcher, Last House on the Left, The Shining, Psycho, Halloween . . .

"Listen, Mr.—" Her voice stalls. His name—his name. What *is* his name? Shit. It's become one of those missing pieces. She can't even remember what it starts with . . . an *M*? Or an *N*?

Sensing the reason for her hesitation, the man laughs. "That's right," he says. "Ellie changed it. Couldn't let her kids be Mitchels, could she?"

"Listen, Mr. Mitchel—"

"Dan," he corrects her. The informality of it makes her feel more uncomfortable.

"Mr. Mitchel," she continues carefully—navigating his presence the way you would navigate cracking ice beneath your feet, "I'm sorry, but . . . you need to leave."

He crouches down low, eye level with Ben, and cocks his head to the side. "You remember me?"

Ben's arm, now wrapped across Amy's entire leg, tightens around her thigh. He doesn't say anything, but Amy can tell by the way Mr. Mitchel is looking at the boy that Ben is looking straight back at him.

What would Nancy do? Or Sadie? Or even Annie? What would Laurie Strode do if someone came looking for little Tommy? "You are not allowed to be here." Amy announces this firmly but politely, as if it is a fact of which Mr. Mitchel had previously not been aware. She hates herself for the way it sounds, almost as much as she hates having said something so obvious. Is this really the best she can do? Possibly. It's taking everything in her to speak clearly and concisely. To keep the words from rattling around in her mouth. To keep the darkness from creeping in. She clenches her fists in an attempt to keep them still—or at least give them the appearance of being still. She feels like she's about ready to throw up—perhaps she should. It might startle him and make him leave.

Right?

Unlikely.

Mr. Mitchel jumps to his feet, and startled herself, Amy finds her heels slipping back across the floor. "These are *my* kids." He takes one step forward, then another, tapping his chest with two lean fingers. "*My* kids, you get that? I don't have to listen to you or anybody else about *my* kids."

One of Amy's fists unravels, her hand subsequently falling across Ben's collarbone—pushing gently at him to get behind her as they back their way into the kitchen. Because even with all her jumbled panic—even with this overwhelming, impetuous fear—it's nothing compared to what he's experiencing. It can't be.

Suddenly, Ben stops moving and she realizes it's because the back of his head has come up against the kitchen counter. The front door feels miles away, but so does the back door. Eleanor's baseball bat is in the laundry room, a place that might as well be on another planet. Amy could scream, but sound has fled her throat—because the man is too close now. And because there's something mixed in with the cigarette smell on him. Whiskey, maybe. She should never have opened the door. What kind of no-good, piece-of-shit teenager opens a stranger's door in the middle of the night? She shouldn't have assumed it was Mr. Darren again. She shouldn't have been so preoccupied with Miles and waiting for a damn apology.

Dan Mitchel squints, and whether it's because he can't see straight or he's trying to scare her, Amy can't tell. The latter is working, though. And she can feel Ben's body shaking behind her.

"Ellie can move away," Mr. Mitchel sneers, "and change their name. Pretend like she was never just a knocked-up rock-star wannabe going nowhere, but *they* are half *me* too. And she'd do best to remember that."

Inhaling and exhaling through her nose, Amy realizes her teeth are clenched so tightly the joints of her jaw are just about screaming with pain. She looks hard into Mr. Mitchel's amber eyes, resolving not to cry. Not to flinch. Praying to God she doesn't faint. Because someone like this'll string you up by your weaknesses if you let them. And she will *not* let him.

His eyes are gleaming in the way a villain's eyes must always gleam— deep and dark and quiet; backlit only by the ardency of his intention. And what *is* his intention? Does he think he will leave with Ben and Mira? Certainly not. How could he? But he waited for Eleanor to be out. He wanted his intrusion to go uncontested. In response to this notion, Amy stands up just about as straight as she can. She readjusts the way her shoulders rest, realizing slowly that she doesn't actually know how to project a sense of authority. And so she tosses out an order, one that is clearly overcompensating in volume. "Get out!"

His face is so close her own breath crashes back against her cheeks. All onions and stale air. "Come out here, B," he says, eyes still locked with Amy's. The boy remains rooted behind her. "I said come out here, boy."

Ben doesn't move. Amy's hands remain curved behind her in an attempt to shield the child.

"Boy!" he orders.

"Dad!" comes a shout in return, only not from Ben. He's now softly crying. Amy can hear it. Nonetheless, the word shoots like a flare across the house. Bright and startling. At first, Amy isn't even sure where it's come from, but when Mr. Mitchel turns around, they both see Mira's small body silhouetted in the hallway.

The girl's father watches, then takes a step toward her, and Mira's fingers begin to tremble. "I called the police," she announces. "They're on their way."

Something in Mr. Mitchel's voice changes, lowering but hardening at the same time. "Baby girl."

"I told them you're in violation of the restraining order," she continues, features steady. Voice firm.

Nearly ready to double over in panic, Amy seizes this moment—when Mr. Mitchel is not looking at her—and leaps across the kitchen with cartoonish urgency. The act of tearing herself from Ben's grip is almost physically painful. Like a betrayal. He's exposed now—he's exposed and he's scared—but she can't think about that. She can't.

In her socks she slides across the floor into the laundry room, knocking down a mop and a package of paper towels as she yanks back the door and pulls out the baseball bat—the one Eleanor had showed her the very first night she'd watched the kids.

"If you're still here when they arrive, they are going to arrest you," Mira says, as Amy topples back into the kitchen beside Ben.

Mr. Mitchel shakes his head. "You really are your ma's little bitch, aren't you?"

"Enough!" Amy snaps, brandishing the bat. She doesn't need to look at Ben to hear that he is crying fully now—no longer trying to hide it—whimpering like a pup left out in the rain. "Mr. Mitchel," she declares, squeezing the handle tightly like she's just stepped up to the plate. Not that she knows the first thing about how to hold it, hoping she's doing it right. Whitney used to play softball—Amy even saw a game or two—but she was never really paying much attention to the hitters. "I think you should leave. Now."

The man shuffles around, feet sliding unevenly. He's probably too drunk to be driving, but Amy doesn't care what he does next. She doesn't care—so long as he walks out that door and she gets to lock it behind him. "Who are you?" he asks, as if seeing her for the first time. He doesn't seem to register the presence of the bat. "Who are *you* to tell *me* where I should be and when I should be there?"

"Do you really want to deal with the cops?"

"Girlie"—he grins wickedly, a villain, indeed—"I've been dealing with 'em since before your tits grew in."

Amy closes the space between them, the line of her mouth set firmly, her sweaty hands gripped tightly around the bat handle—both desperate for and terrified at the very possibility of swinging. "And you really want your kids to watch them drag you out of here?"

He gestures at the bat. "There's no way Ellie's paying you enough for this."

Amy takes a few steps back, leveling her stance. "Varsity softball," she says, gritting her teeth. "*Try me.*"

He doesn't back down right away, but he looks as if he might. And that's good enough for Amy. And so, she waits . . . and waits . . . and waits . . . unblinking. Unfeeling. Unable to breathe. Until, finally, Mr. Mitchel laughs and shakes his head and mutters a series of words Ben's too young to be hearing. He shuffles reluctantly in the direction of the door, and as he enters the hallway, Mira turns sharply to avoid him. He stops and she looks away. "Definitely your mother's little bitch," he grumbles again, almost under his breath, and as he stumbles out the door, Amy rushes to slam it shut behind him.

Turning the lock tightly in place, she spins around to face the kids and her back falls loudly against the door. The baseball bat clatters to the floor. She allows herself one deep, shaky breath before hurrying back into the kitchen and kneeling in front of Ben. She was right, he's crying—or was. His cheeks are wet and his eyes are red, but he seems to have stopped. "Are you all right?" she asks, running her fingers through his hair and down across his shoulders and arms, clutching his hands tightly in her own. "Look at me. Are you okay?"

He nods wordlessly, stare pinned snugly to the floor. When Amy turns to find Mira, she sees that the girl is still standing in between the hallway and the living room, her face quite pale. She's scratching desperately at her wrist.

"Mira! Are you all right?"

Mira's hands are shaking more violently now, and in a feeble attempt to calm them, she shoves both under her arms.

"Mira!"

The girl looks up at her, head low between her shoulders, eyes wide like she's just been slapped across the face. Slapped one too many times.

Amy frowns. "He's gone," she assures her. "You hear me? He's gone."

Taking Ben by the hand, she leads him into the living room. When they get there, he doesn't want to let her go, and so Amy uses her free hand to touch Mira's arm. The girl flinches at the gesture.

"Hey," Amy murmurs softly. "Easy . . . easy . . . look at me," she hums. "Mira, look at me."

Mira's gaze rises to meet her own, and for Amy it is like looking into the eyes of the dead. She shudders, pulling Ben close.

"Listen to me," she says. "Everything is going to be all right. I promise."

Something in Mira's expression falters, and it's like Amy's presence before her finally comes into focus. "You can't promise that," she says flatly.

The babysitter frowns, running her fingers through Ben's hair again. Only he isn't watching them anymore. He's looking at the TV—still paused on Michael Myers with the sheet over his head.

Ben frowns. "Is that the ghost?" he asks.

Amy shakes her head, rising quickly to her feet and grabbing the remote off the couch. She presses stop and eject. The VCR groans before spitting out the VHS. "No," she insists. "Of course not. Now come on, it's getting late."

CHAPTER THIRTEEN

BEN

FRIDAY, OCTOBER 15, 1993

5:05 P.M. (6 HOURS AND 55 MINUTES BEFORE MIDNIGHT)

Slowly, M draws the polish across the nail of her big toe. A steady line of red.

"You're lying," says Ben.

She shrugs. "Why would I even bother?"

Ben doesn't know the answer to this and so he just sits and watches as his sister blots the edge of the nail with a piece of toilet paper.

"But last time you said it was from falling outside," he complains. "How can it be from falling *and* from getting bitten by a dog?"

"Maybe I fell running from the dog and then it bit me," she suggests, only Ben doesn't buy it. M loves dogs. Would never say a bad word against one, even if that bad word happened to be true. She's had the little tiny scars all around her foot and ankle for as long as he can remember. And every time he asks her how she got them M comes up with a completely different explanation. Rusty nail on the stairs. Jumping rope. Dropping scissors. Fighting pirates. Any of these could be true, except maybe for the last one. Because Ben is pretty sure his sister has never met any pirates.

Having just touched up the third toe from the right, M leans back to examine her work in full. She drops the toilet paper into the toilet behind her and twists closed the top of the nail polish. She holds the bottle up to him. "Want me to do yours?"

Ben shakes his head. Mom paints his toenails all the time. Usually black. Sometimes pink or blue. It takes forever to come off but he likes the attention Mom pays him while she uses the brush. They have some of their best talks then. M can't make fun of anything he says while Mom is painting his nails because she always spends that time in her room. It means he gets Mom all to himself. And Ben likes that.

M sighs and, twisting around, drops the polish back into the second drawer on the left below the sink, the one filled with different liners and lipsticks and old eye shadows Mom barely ever uses anymore. M tried something called mascara one time, but it made her eyelids itch. She's always testing out different eye shadows and lipsticks, though. She claims she's looking for her exact right shade. Every girl needs a signature shade. That's what Aunt Patty says.

Sliding makeup around inside the drawer, M pulls out two lipsticks and examines each name closely. She looks at Ben. "Dark Velvet or New Rose?"

Ben's shoulders rise and fall indifferently.

Examining the tubes again, M tosses one back in the drawer and opens the other—New Rose, he thinks. She twists the bottom until a soft stick of color rises up. Grabbing the compact off the floor beside her, she pops it open and looks into the tiny little mirror, chipped in the corner, as she traces her mouth with the lipstick. It adds a soft coloring to her thin lips, creamy like paint but not as thick. When she's finished, M leans back and rolls her lips like a fish before grabbing another sheet of toilet paper and doing something called blotting. Mom explained it to him one time. It's supposed to make the color look less thick, more natural.

As Mira throws the rose-printed sheet of toilet paper into the bowl behind her, she returns her attention to the mirror.

"Too pink?" she asks, tilting her head curiously.

"No."

"Good."

Returning the compact and the lipstick to the drawer, M stretches before spreading her palms flat across the gray-tiled floor. She wriggles her toes, impatient for them to dry. Mom is the same way—restless. Bored. Convinced that simply wanting them to dry will somehow speed the process along.

It's probably why Mom is terrible at keeping secrets. Or not secrets exactly—surprises. Mom loves surprises, but she has trouble waiting to surprise anyone. It's why her friends don't let her plan surprise parties. She's always giving her kids birthday gifts the night before. "This is how our people do it," she insists, because Jewish holidays start the night before. Only Mom gives them Chanukah presents early too—a day or two before the night on which they are supposed to start lighting candles. It's just that Mom gets so excited about things—rushing straight ahead into the future, the past scrambling to catch up with her.

Last weekend, she woke them at five in the morning to watch the sun rise. She said it was supposed to be a beautiful one and she didn't want them to miss it. Only the sun wasn't even supposed to come up for a couple of hours. Mom was so excited—she coaxed them out of bed and made hot chocolate and had M help her turn the couch around so that it would face the big window in the living room. She pulled open the blinds and the three of them sat there drinking hot chocolate and watching the sky slowly turn gray, then purple, then pink, and, eventually, blue. She told them life is filled with beautiful moments, and if they didn't grab those moments then they'd float away. Like clouds. Gone forever. She usually sounds a little sad when she says things like this, but not on that day with the sunrise. On that morning she was bright and hopeful and maybe just a little bit magic. Ben is convinced there are times when his mother is pure magic. There's no other way to describe the things she does. The things she says. The way she makes him feel safe.

Ben's attention falls across M's hands, the blotchy red print across her knuckles. "Are you hitting doors again?" he asks, because he knows Mom has already questioned her about it. Not that M told her anything. M used to hit doors at the apartment when she got really, really mad. She'd go to the big front door because it was made of metal and wouldn't dent. She'd close her eyes and scrunch her fists up tight and hurl one into the door as hard as she could. Usually, she did it just one time. Sometimes, if she was really mad, she'd do it twice. Hitting that door must have hurt her hand, though, because her knuckles were always bright red afterward. One time they even bled.

"No," she responds flatly. "I'm not hitting doors."

"Then what did you hit?"

She rolls her tongue around her mouth, thinking it over.

"What did you hit?"

After a few moments she mutters "Matt Foster's face" in an irritable but matter-of-fact way that suggests this is the beginning and the end of the conversation. She says it as if he might have guessed this himself had she not gone ahead and told him. Only, as far as Ben knows, his sister has never hit anyone before.

Ben wonders if she's lying. It doesn't sound like a lie. Most of the time she looks right at him when she lies, and right now, she's just staring at the tiled floor, trying very hard not to look at him. Maybe this means she's telling the truth.

"Why?" he asks.

She shrugs, glancing at him for half a second before averting her gaze again. "He called Mom a stripper."

"What's a stripper?"

"Someone who takes their clothes off in front of other people."

Ben's brow creases. He doesn't see how this is wrong. Mom used to change in front of them all the time back at the apartment, when the rooms were so small she had to keep her dresser in the living room.

"In front of strangers," M clarifies, because he must not look upset enough. At this, he tilts his head.

"Why would she do that?"

"She doesn't," M assures him. "But Matt Foster was saying she should because his dad said he'd pay good money to see her naked."

"That's why you hit him?"

M nods quietly.

"And you didn't get in trouble?"

"Trouble?" M nearly snickers. "Like he would ever admit he was punched by a girl. Mr. Harley didn't see, so when Matt's nose started bleeding, he said he walked into the locker-room door."

Ben's eyes widen. "You made his nose bleed?"

M nods, almost proud. Then she looks sternly at her little brother. "We don't let people say things like that about Mom. Understand?"

He nods, even though he's still not sure what exactly it was the boy in her class was saying. He recognizes M's tone though—the low, serious rumble of her certainty. For a moment M studies his face, assessing the extent of his agreement. He tries to sit up straight. Look grown-up, like her. Shaking her head, M cautiously looks back at her feet and touches the very tip of a toenail, frowning when it leaves a little red smudge along her skin.

"It's not dry yet," Ben tells her.

His sister only scowls.

"Were you?" he asks.

"Was I what?"

"Running from a dog," he says, but he must not look very convinced because M turns her head at him and laughs.

"You wouldn't believe me if I told you."

"Yes, I would."

"No, you wouldn't," she argues defiantly. "You'd call me a liar."

He thinks she's lying now, but he doesn't say this. He just gazes down at her toes, wondering if she's going to fix the one she smeared.

"Does Mom tell you everything?" M asks him suddenly.

Looking up, Ben thinks about this, then nods.

M reaches to retrieve the nail polish from the drawer, picking up and tossing back different shades of purple and blue and green until she finds the one she'd been using before. She shakes the bottle and unscrews the top. "Nope," she says, eyes fixed on the brush as she pulls it out and gently slips it across that marred toenail. "Wrong. She doesn't. So why should I?"

"That's not true."

"You think she's honest with you all the time?"

"Mom doesn't lie."

"She doesn't have to, B. It's called lying by omission," she explains. He doesn't know what *omission* means or what it has to do with lying, but he nods like he does so M will think he's smart.

His sister laughs. "Mom only tells you what she thinks you can hear."

Ben's muscles tense. This makes him mad, not at the idea that Mom is keeping things from him, but at the thought of M knowing more about her than he does. It's like she and Mom belong to a club he's not allowed into. An all-girl club where boys are bad and grow up to be badder. It's not his fault he's not like them, is it?

"I just wanna know how you got the scars," he admits helplessly. His eyes burn. Maybe he'll start to cry. But he doesn't want to do that—not in front of M. She never cries.

"I already told you."

"M . . ."

Having thoroughly examined her work, M pretends to be busy closing the cap on the nail polish.

"Please."

"No!"

"But I won't tell anyone," Ben pleads.

He's ready for her to start shouting at him—that's what she usually does when he refuses to let something go—but she surprises him. Instead of getting annoyed, M smiles, tracing the line of his cheek with her forefinger. The whole bathroom smells and tastes like nail polish, but she likes it. Always has. His head is starting to hurt from the smell. "When did you get to be so nosy, huh?" she asks. "Do you know?"

He shakes his head.

"Exactly. Because sometimes things just happen. And we don't remember when or why. We just know that they did."

She shoves the bottle into his hands, and reluctantly, Ben returns the bottle to the drawer. M slams the drawer shut, sighing again. Only this time she doesn't seem quite so impatient.

She nudges his leg with her heel and he looks at her again. "Are you sure the lipstick isn't too pink?"

"No. I like it."

This seems to please his sister, because she smiles. "Good. Now grab me the eyelash curler."

CHAPTER FOURTEEN

AMY

FRIDAY, OCTOBER 15, 1993
9:45 P.M. (2 HOURS AND 15 MINUTES BEFORE MIDNIGHT)

Mira comes into the room with a glass of water from the kitchen and passes it to her brother. Ben, who has not said a word since their father left, reluctantly releases Amy's hands and accepts the glass between his warm, sticky palms.

"Thank you," murmurs Amy, to which Mira does not respond. She just stands there watching her brother not drinking while Amy kneels alongside the couch, watching him watch her watch him not drink his water. "It will be all right," Amy assures him, though she's lost track of how many times she's said this now. Two? Eight? Twelve? The words feel as if they are starting to dull in her mouth.

Blinking aimlessly at the glass in his hand, Ben eventually leans forward in an attempt to put it on the coffee table. Mira intercepts the glass and takes a long gulp before placing it on the table and turning to Amy. "Can we go now?"

The babysitter looks at her. "The police will probably want to talk to you when they get here."

"They're not coming."

"What?"

"No one's coming."

"Why not?"

"I didn't call them," says Mira, staring back at her blankly.

Amy frowns. What if Mr. Mitchel waits? What if he comes back and calls their bluff? Mira steals a glance at her brother, and it takes Amy a few minutes to realize that Mira is not trying to conjure up an explanation. She's waiting to be excused. "Mira . . ." she urges, but the girl refuses to relent. Stubborn, even after all of this. Maybe *because* of all that's happened. Against every instinct in her body, Amy doesn't press the matter any further. She exhales through her nose. Her shoulders slump helplessly. "You . . . can go upstairs, if you want."

Mira doesn't stick around for Amy to change her mind or for her brother to gather up the strength to follow her. She just leaves the room and marches upstairs and slams the bedroom door behind her. At the sound of it, Ben jumps—startled—and Amy takes hold of his hand again.

"You want to stay with me for a bit?" she asks him.

Ben nods, his gaze falling on the near-empty glass on the table.

Amy smiles. "How about I get you some more water? Then maybe we can find a good book to read."

The corners of his lips curve upward, as if he might just smile, and cautiously the boy lets go of her hand, which by now is sweaty and warm and very, very tense. Amy grabs the glass, and as she does so Ben retrieves something from his pocket—a few folded-up pages—and offers it to her. Amy takes them, recognizing the familiar red print of the book fair catalogue. "Did you pick some out?" she asks.

He nods.

Flipping through as best she can with one hand, Amy examines the pages. A few of the books have been double-circled in blue marker—one on the back and three on page 2. "Nice, I like those dog books." She nods approvingly. "Where should we put this? On the fridge? So your mom will see it?"

Ben relinquishes another nod.

Amy takes the catalogue with her into the kitchen and places it on the island as she refills his glass at the sink. It's here, in the moments after shutting off the water and before turning around completely, that she notices the magnets on the refrigerator. They've abandoned their rounded shape, now situated in a somewhat crooked horizontal line. She chews on her bottom lip, leaning in as if her proximity has somehow triggered an illusion.

Only, no—it's true. The magnets *have* moved.

But when?

There is no such thing as ghosts, she reminds herself. *The Mazinski house is not haunted.*

Watch, now she's probably going to round the corner and come face-to-face with a malevolent spirit.

Who is more ridiculous: the girl who believes scary movie cues or the girl who ignores them?

Amy is starting to feel damned either way, and rolling her shoulders up and down to loosen the joints, she returns to the living room. "So," she says, handing Ben the glass. "What should we read?"

The little boy drinks, then shrugs, then drinks some more. Tight, tiny sips.

Amy looks around the room, hands on her hips. "Where do you keep your books?"

"Upstairs," he answers, the word small and meek in his mouth. Nonetheless, it's a comfort to hear him speak at all—to know his father's sudden manifestation has not sucked every last word from him. She smiles and he mirrors her by smiling back.

Amy nods in the direction of the stairs. "Should we go have a look then?"

Ben's head bobs up and down. She waits for him to finish his water and, when the glass is empty, she takes it and sets it down on the table.

He gently slips his hand into her hand and they head upstairs in smooth, taut silence.

This is all her fault. She was the one who let their father into the house. She'll have to tell Eleanor about it—of course she will. And what will Eleanor think? She'll be angry, surely. Amy would be angry if some babysitter allowed *her* drunken ex to come barging in to scare the kids.

And what would she have done if Mira hadn't threatened him with the police? Could Amy have gotten rid of him on her own? She wants to think that she would have come up with something, but it's astonishing how panic—pure and precise and pungent panic—manages to strip her of any and all instincts. What if he had insisted on staying? What if he had tried to take the kids with him?

Amy could hate herself for having been so completely, utterly useless.

In the upstairs hallway, the babysitter wriggles her hand free from Ben's fingers and points to his open bedroom door. "Why don't you decide which one you want to read? I want to check on your sister real quick."

The boy stays put, uncertainty heavy in his heels.

Amy smiles encouragingly. "It will just be a minute. I promise."

She watches as the boy hesitates, frowns, and does exactly as she's requested. Then she knocks on Mira's door.

Unsurprisingly, she is met with silence.

She knocks again.

"What?" Mira calls out.

"Can I talk to you for a second?"

There is a long, tenuous pause before she answers.

"Why?"

"I just want to talk."

More silence, then: "Whatever."

It's not a yes, but it's not exactly a no either. Amy waits for Mira to come to the door, but when she doesn't the babysitter opens it herself, the hinges sighing with a high little *creak*. Mira is lying on her bed, a notebook spread open in front of her.

"Hey," says Amy, taking a few more steps forward across the green carpet. It's the first time she's ever been this far into the girl's room, and she notices suddenly how it smells, ever so slightly, of Eleanor's lavender perfume. Flowery and fragrant. "How are you doing?"

Mira shrugs. "Fine."

"Yeah?"

Mira looks down at her notebook. About a page and a half is filled with scribbled text, though Amy is too far away to read any of it. Mira's handwriting doesn't exactly encourage her to try.

"You know, I was a little scared back there," she says, hoping it will draw Mira out. Only it has the opposite effect. The admission causes the girl's lips to purse, as if she's disappointed that Amy could be so easily shaken.

The babysitter pauses, then tries a new tactic. "I think the ghost is at it again," she redirects, folding her arms. It's warmer upstairs than it is downstairs, but the house is pretty chilly overall. She can't tell if it's because the place is poorly insulated or because Eleanor keeps the thermostat low. She'll have to check when she goes back to the living room. She shouldn't forget what Ben said, that sometimes you have to hit it.

"All the magnets on the fridge," Amy continues. "They've been moved around."

Mira remains committed to *not* looking at Amy and *not* letting on that she's tempted to look at her, subsequently failing at both. Her gaze slowly slips up and across Amy's face. The babysitter's hands begin to fidget as she turns that ring round and round her finger. The silence between them stretches until it is long and thin and just about ready to snap. "You're the ghost," says Amy. "Aren't you?"

This time Mira does look at her, their eyes locking in one pure and precise instant of complete understanding. As if it's the first time either one of them is laying eyes on the other.

"That's right, isn't it?" Amy continues. "You're the ghost who's been moving everything."

Mira's fingers perch tensely against edge of her notebook.

"You haven't told your brother?"

Ever so slightly, the girl shakes her head.

"Why not?"

Mira's forefinger traces the outline of the notebook, one, two, six times. Biting on the inside of her cheek, she keeps her eyes fastened to the open pages in front of her. "He's safer scared," she says at last. "And that's good. We're all safer if we're scared."

Amy sticks her tongue to the inside of her cheek, then exhales deeply. "Are you scared?"

Mira shrugs.

"Your dad's not coming back," she assures her, as if this is a promise she can make. Only they both know Amy has no power in this department. The promise is as good as a lie. Mira scratches her wrist.

"Bottle caps," she says. "He liked to throw bottle caps. And matches. Not at B, just at me. When Mom wasn't around. Then one day she was around and B was hungry and crying and I wanted something—I don't remember what. I was screaming and he was screaming and our dad . . . he hit me."

Mira's hand doesn't go to her cheek here. She digs her nails into her wrist, and Amy wants to stop her but she's afraid to touch the girl—afraid to shake her.

"Mom lost it," the girl continues. "Started pushing him. Throwing things. Shouting. She tried to hurl a bottle at his head, but it missed and hit the floor. He grabbed her and I thought he was going to kill her so I—I tried to pull him off."

Sliding her leg out from beneath her, Mira exposes one of her bare feet to reveal a constellation of scarring near her ankle. "He grabbed me by the hair and dragged me through the broken bottle pieces. Threw me in the closet and closed the door. Told Mom he wouldn't let me out until she apologized."

Amy does not say anything, because if she does, she knows her voice will crack and it wouldn't be fair if she was to start crying now. Because Mira's cheeks are bone dry. And her voice is very calm. And her eyes are very patient.

At last, Mira pulls her fingers from her wrist, revealing a set of nail-shaped indents. "He's bad," says Mira. "Ben doesn't remember because he was too small, but our dad is bad. And that's why our mom left him."

Amy always considered herself to have a strong stomach—but not for this. Not for real violence. Against real children. "I'm so sorry he came here." The words feel inadequate for what she wants to convey. And yet she says them anyway. Just to say something. Anything. She doesn't want Mira to think she's not listening, or that she doesn't care.

The girl touches the pen lying in the middle of her notebook, tracing it from bottom to top to bottom again with her forefinger. "If I really had called the police, they would have wanted to call our mom," she explains. "And she would have had to come home."

"Mira, she'd be upset, but not at you—not because she'd be coming home to you."

"She's spent a lot of time being unhappy," Mira continues. "She deserves a good time. Even if my brother doesn't like it. She's happier when she gets to go out."

"You shouldn't have to worry about your mom."

"Then who will?"

Amy blinks back at her, lost for words. Instead of waiting for an answer, Mira slips back onto her belly, pulling the notebook close as she resumes her writing.

"You can leave," she says, not looking up.

Amy frowns. "Mira—"

"Ben doesn't like to be alone."

Amy tries to put a hand on Mira's shoulder, but the girl only pivots away. It makes Amy uneasy. Because Mira is hurting. And it's obvious she's hurting. And there is nothing Amy can think to do about it. She wants to stay, to do something—but what?

"Your mom won't let him come back."

Startled, Mira looks up and frowns. Unconvinced.

"She won't," Amy assures her. "She'll make sure he stays away."

"How?"

"I don't know, but she will. Because you were very brave tonight. And you were strong for your brother. And you had to have gotten those traits from somewhere. My bet is that you're a lot like your mom."

Something akin to uncertainty ripples across Mira's face.

"You're actually sort of terrifying when you want to be," Amy adds. "Trust me."

A smirk, faint and fading, crosses Mira's lips. The girl nods like she understands, like she might even believe what Amy's telling her, before looking back down at her notebook.

Amy hesitates, tempted to try to catch a glimpse of what Mira had written. She stands and goes to leave, stopping halfway across the room to watch the girl as she writes. Then Amy moves out into the hallway, closing the door behind her.

In Ben's room she finds the little boy sitting on the floor by the wall, piles of hardcover picture books and flimsy little chapter books stacked in front of him. They all have library stickers on the spines, worn white labels with finely printed barcodes. "Find something good?" she asks.

Ben stops and scoops up three of the books, while Amy grabs the two left on the floor. "Should we read all of them?"

Relief settles across his face. As if he'd been worried that she might not want to commit so much time to him. "Yeah."

Ben takes a seat on the bed and Amy joins him, drawing the first book, one about a dinosaur looking for a party, into her lap. She opens it to the title page, but Ben isn't looking at the book. He's too busy looking at the carpet like he's trying to burn a hole in it. Creating a crater in which to hide. She places a hand on his shoulder and he trembles under her touch.

"Is she mad?" he asks quietly.

"Who?"

"M."

"What? No—no, she's not mad at you."

Shame lends a certain paleness to his cheeks, his skin so soft and thin she can just about see the veins spread out underneath like a map stretched across his brow.

"She said not to pick up the phone," Ben says.

Amy tries to draw him closer to her, but his small form—no longer trembling—remains rigid. Eventually, she coaxes him into leaning along the curve of her arm. "You know, I always wanted a big sister," she tells him. "I don't have any sisters. Or brothers."

He looks up. "Why not?"

She shrugs. "Don't know. My parents just wanted one, I guess. I've got, I think, like, sixteen cousins, but no siblings. Just me."

His head sinks like that of a punished puppy. "M wishes Mom had just her."

"No—that's not true. Maybe she didn't want a brother before you were born, but that's because she was little. And she hadn't met you yet. But now she loves you. That's what big sisters do."

He responds with an unconvinced half shrug.

"Hey, listen to me. She was mad at your dad for coming here, and maybe she was a little scared for you, but she wasn't mad at you. You're her little brother. She wants to look out for you. And you will always have each other. That's what's so great about it."

A tiny tinge of envy catches in Amy's throat. She has friends and family and Miles but she still feels alone most of the time. All of the time. Even Charlie and Donnie are too busy with girlfriends and work and student loans to go to the movies with her anymore. Then there are the panic attacks that never seem to go away—her one true constant.

"I get scared too sometimes," she admits quietly, her chin resting on the top of his head.

He pulls away a little, just to get a better look at her face, as if her expression might betray the words and prove she's lying.

"What?" she says. "It's true."

"Really?"

"Yeah. All the time. Ever since I was little. Sometimes I'm so scared I can't breathe, and then I just get even more scared." Ben studies her expression carefully, waiting for her to say more—to give him answers, perhaps. Only her mind is drawing a stark blank.

"It's the Fear," he tells her quietly.

"What's that?"

"The Fear," he repeats, unfazed. "We've always had the Fear."

"We?"

"M and me."

"Oh."

She lets the word, which is really just a sound, languish somewhere between them. Ben doesn't say anything. He's about the age she was when she had her first panic attack. The first one she can recall, anyway. It wasn't anything particularly striking. Just an afternoon in Whitney's backyard. They were up in the tree house and Whitney had this caterpillar and she wanted Amy to hold it, but Amy was too afraid and Whitney tried to put it on her arm anyway. Amy drew back, stumbled, and fell out of the treehouse. She landed on the grass a few feet below—not even a great distance—but lying there on her back she suddenly couldn't breathe. Her chest ached. Every signal in her brain told her to run, but she couldn't. She couldn't move. Whitney ran to get her mom, but by the time they got back it was all over. Amy was breathing normally again, and the tightness between her ribs was gone.

The Mazinski kids have had to endure much more than rogue caterpillars, and for this Amy concedes to self-loathing. It is, essentially, her natural default. Her fear is nothing in comparison with what they have been through. Her fear is strong, yes, but false. A misfiring of signals in her brain. It doesn't mean anything. Whereas with Dan Mitchel, and the story Mira had told, and the terror in Ben's eyes when his father looked at him—that was real. That was danger. How do you protect a child from the past? Experience and trauma cannot be coaxed, threatened, thrown out. They're more complicated than that. They imprint themselves on the brain. Scrawled across the soul in memory.

"You know, there are things you can do," she tells him. "When you're scared, there are ways to make yourself less scared."

"How?"

Amy takes his hands and holds them up to mirror her own. "You squeeze your hands tight into fists like this," she explains, slowly balling her fingers up tight. Ben does the same. "And you keep on squeezing as hard as you can. Then, when your fingers feel like they're gonna break, you let go."

She opens her hands flat again. Ben opens his.

"And you just keep doing it again and again and again until you're not so scared anymore."

Amy watches Ben squeeze his hands into a fist and loosen them, squeeze and loosen them over and over until his eyes don't seem quite as wary as they had before.

"Very good," she says with a smile, and true to his very nature, the boy smiles back. "And, you know, when you're all done with that there are always these books you've got here. There is nothing on this earth a good book and a good glass of milk can't solve. So how about we read until our eyes pop. Then I will get you a warm glass of milk and sit with you until you fall asleep. What do you say?"

"You don't have to sit with me," he assures her. "I'm not scared of the dark."

Amy knows from last time that this isn't true. She tilts her head. "You're not?"

"No," he manages a little undecidedly.

"Really? Because I am."

"You are?"

She nods. "I like to leave a lamp on at night."

He hesitates, wrestling with the truth. "Me too."

"Yeah? Well, we can leave a lamp on then, even if you don't want me to sit with you. Okay?"

Without saying a word, Ben leans his head against her arm. And taking this as a sign of agreement, she turns to the first page of the first book and begins to read.

They stood at the door of her parents' bedroom like Indiana Jones approaching the Temple of the Chachapoyan Warriors. Amy dug her big toe into the carpet. "I'm not supposed to," she said.

Sadie smiled that warm, pretty, reassuring smile. "It's what my sister and I always did at your age when our mom was out."

Amy considered this but remained silent.

"You don't want to watch a movie or play a game," Sadie reminded her. It was true. Having gotten through the math, Amy's eyes hurt and she didn't really feel like doing much of anything. Kids were supposed to be energetic at her age, but not her.

She wasn't budging and so Sadie placed a hand on Amy's shoulder and opened the door herself. The room smelled fresh, with the floral Estée Lauder perfume Amy's mother had spritzed on before leaving for the night. Sadie switched on the light and Amy's bare feet tingled as she shuffled across the shag carpet to the closet. Next to the closet stood the jewelry armoire Aunt Debra had given to Amy's mother as a wedding present.

"Now, your ears aren't pierced, are they?" said Sadie, feeling at Amy's unpunctured lobes for confirmation. She paused with a thoughtful expression on her face, brow pinched and lips twisted to one side. Then she opened the armoire and bent down to peer inside. Brushing a lock of blond hair from her face, she reached for a sapphire-studded gold pendant Amy's mother liked to wear to holiday parties. "Let's try this one," said Sadie. "I think the blue will look beautiful with your hair." She fastened the necklace around Amy's throat, straightened the pendant, and smiled again. "There! Take a look."

Amy turned to the full-length mirror in the corner of the room and looked at herself. She knew every curve of the face that stared back at her, the way her cheekbones weren't as pronounced as she wanted them to be, and how her eyebrows were just a little too bushy to be shapely. But Sadie was right. The sapphires did look beautiful. They were deep and dark and sparkled in the light as she shifted her weight. Before she knew it, she was smiling at herself—not smiling to scrutinize the way her cheeks bunched up when she did so, but smiling a real, genuine smile that glowed softly with delight.

"This would look fabulous with a bracelet." Sadie turned back to the armoire. "Something delicate . . ."

Amy picked up a large two-tone ring, the one her mother had gotten in Cape May when her family went to the beach last summer. Amy liked the grooves in the hammered metal, the weight of it heavy in her palm.

"Here!" Sadie pulled a thin gold chain from one of the velvet-lined compartments and gestured for Amy's wrist. Amy obliged, putting the ring back and allowing Sadie to put the bracelet on her and do the clasp. It was a little big on Amy's child-size wrist and she jingled her arm to watch it move. It was so lightweight, almost like wearing nothing at all.

Sadie leaned back, hands on her hips, as she examined the reflection of her handiwork in the mirror. "Aw, you look pretty!" she squealed approvingly.

Amy glanced up at her with such shock in her face she almost seemed alarmed. "Do I?"

"Absolutely." Sadie petted the girl's hair, tucking it behind Amy's ears as she smoothed it. "I still think you should consider bangs, though," she added with a giggle, tossing the girl a wink.

Amy gazed at her own mirrored reflection with wonder. Maybe she'd ask her mother about getting bangs. Only, at the thought of her mother—her parents—it dawned on her again that they were in this room, trying on her mother's things. She was only allowed to do this when her mother was around. She'd been told so on more than one occasion.

Suddenly the little thrill she'd begun to feel went sour in her chest. That ballooning feeling in her belly returned, and her vision blurred the way hot pavement burns went you look out at it on a sunny day. Amy stumbled back, nearly falling into Sadie's arms.

"Hey, hey—what's the matter?" asked Sadie. Amy opened her mouth, but all the words rushed up her throat at once, knotting together. Could she choke on them? Was that possible? "Hey, peanut," Sadie continued, kneeling in front of Amy and staring steadily into her eyes. "It's okay. You're okay. Do you hear me? Nod it you understand."

Amy nodded.

"Good, here . . ." She took Amy's hands into her own. "Let's breathe in and out, okay? In and out. Good, good girl. Just like that. And you see here?" Sadie held their hands up between them. Letting go of Amy's, she squeezed her own into fists and then stretched them out, long-fingered. "See how I'm doing this? Try it? Make a fist then push it out." Sadie repeated the motion several times, Amy mirroring it. After a few minutes—maybe more than a few minutes—Amy could feel her heartbeat slowing back down to a reasonable rhythm. "There." Sadie smiled. "See? Sometimes when we get upset, it just means there's energy in our bodies that wants to get out. When you squeeze your hands, you use the energy. And it helps you relax again."

Amy looked up at her, bewildered. As if Sadie had just revealed the secret to the whole wide universe to her. "I have—I have," Amy said, trying to remember the word for it. "A—anxiety." The term still felt strange and unfamiliar in her mouth. Like a new tooth that feels bigger than the one it's come in to replace.

"Anxiety?" Sadie repeated. "Do you know what that means?"

Amy nodded, trying and only half succeeding to remember everything Dr. Somer had told her and her parents about it. For a moment, she felt like she might cry. But she didn't want to do that. Not in front of Sadie.

"Then you know anxiety is just a feeling. Your brain playing tricks on you. We all have something that feels more challenging than it should," Sadie explained. "I don't get anxious like you, but I have a lot of energy. Too much, my sister says. Sometimes I can't help it, I just have to move. That's probably why I like baking so much. It keeps me busy. And if I can't move because I'm in a classroom or a car or something, I do this little trick"—she held up her hand, squeezed it into a fist, and relaxed it again—"to balance myself out. It's a good one, isn't it?"

Amy nodded.

"I think it has something to do with the way it helps you focus," Sadie told her. "For me, it keeps my fidgety hands busy, but for you it might help channel some of that nervous energy."

Amy wondered if Sadie would tell her parents about this, but before she could ask, the babysitter suddenly rose to her feet.

"You know what this outfit needs?" asked Sadie, stroking her chin in mock curiosity.

Amy shrugged.

"A good hat."

Amy hesitated, glancing at the door and squirming like she had to go to the bathroom. "Can we go now?"

Sadie laughed. "What? We just started!"

Amy wanted to try the hand-squeezing thing again, but then Sadie would know she was still uncomfortable. "We're not supposed to be in here."

Sadie exhaled in disappointment, but said nothing. Amy turned to leave when the babysitter grabbed her. Amy jumped with a start. "Do you know what fear does?" Sadie asked. She didn't look unkind, but her face was a little more serious now.

Amy shook her head.

"It controls us," Sadie told her. "The only way to beat fear is to ignore it. Then it's powerless and it can't hurt you." Amy looked down at Sadie's hand and the babysitter's grip loosened. She let go of Amy and tucked a lock of hair behind the little girl's ear. Petted her head affectionately. "Do you want to be afraid?" she asked.

Amy shook her head.

"No. Me neither."

CHAPTER SIXTEEN

BEN

FRIDAY, OCTOBER 15, 1993
3:51 P.M. (8 HOURS AND 9 MINUTES BEFORE MIDNIGHT)

Tearing a piece of thin, sticky fruitiness off the paper, Ben watches the strip dangle before popping it into his mouth. He turns the remaining roll of Fruit by the Foot back and forth in his hands. Pulls off another bite and folds it onto his tongue. He likes the kind Mom got this time—sweet, but a little tart too. Just like real strawberries. The vibrant, almost see-through red reminds him of a tray he saw at Nana's after she'd died. They never went to go see her when she was alive, even though she came to see them at the apartment and sent presents for Chanukah and their birthdays. After she died, they went to her house lots of times to pack things up. Only, by then, she wasn't there anymore.

The tray Nana had, it was all different colors. Very delicate. Stained glass. That's what Mom called it. He remembers because Mom's mom—they don't call her grandma even though he's pretty sure she *is* their grandma—said she wanted it. And Mom didn't want to give it up. And they yelled and yelled and yelled about it one afternoon out front in Nana's yard and Mom was so mad her face turned red and she started to cry. M wasn't home that day. She'd gone with Aunt Patty to get her nails done. If M had been there, she would have known what to do—what to say.

In the end, Mom didn't get to keep the tray, and she was sad—sadder than Ben thought she would be about a little glass tray. When M got back later, he told her all about it. His sister said it wasn't about the tray, it was about Mom and her mom, but Ben wasn't so sure. He thinks she really wanted the tray. He wanted it too. He'd never seen anything so pretty.

He hadn't had a chance to eat his snack with his lunch today. He'd been too busy listening to Steve talk about the time he and his brother filled one Super Soaker with soap and one Super Soaker with water and tried to wash the dog. According to Steve, it didn't really work, and the dog's been terrified of them ever since. Ben's glad he kept his Fruit by the Foot, though, and didn't accidentally throw it away with the rest of his lunch. He did that once and sulked the whole day afterward because it had been the last package in the whole house.

Placing the Fruit by the Foot roll on the napkin next to him, Ben returns to his cards, which are piled very carefully on the kitchen table. Angling the six of spades just so, he leans the two of diamonds gently along its edge. As he lets go of the cards he holds his breath, certain that even the slightest disturbance will knock them flat again. When the cards remain upright, he smiles to himself, pulls off another piece of Fruit by the Foot, and chews happily as he determines where to place the next card. He's not as good at making houses as Aunt Patty—she can make them two stories tall—but he's been practicing. Usually, he can stand about four or five before the entire thing crumbles.

It's as he props the sixth card up that the house falls apart, and, frowning, he stares down at the flat little cards. They look so much smaller this way than they had before. He takes off a piece of fruity deliciousness and assesses his failure as he chews. After swallowing, he pulls off the last piece and presses the end gently between his teeth. Then he goes into the bathroom by the laundry room and turns on the light and looks in the mirror. He smiles. The piece hanging from his lips looks like a very, very long tongue. It even curls a little at the end. Like a lizard tongue.

He slowly slurps up this "tongue" inch by inch until the last bit at the bottom disappears into his mouth. It's juicy and sweet.

Back in the kitchen he piles the cards up evenly and throws the paper from his snack in the garbage before wandering out of the kitchen and into the living room. M is tucked into the far corner of the couch, a book on her knees. He doesn't know the title, but it's the one she started on Wednesday, the cover all red with no pictures. She says it's about a woman and a baby, but won't read it to him. Mom says she used to read to him all the time when she was first learning—every book she could get her hands on. That was when he was a baby, though, and every time he asks her to read now she tells him to go away.

Standing patiently at the edge of the room, Ben eyes the remote on the couch by his sister's feet. He knows she'll holler at him if he tries to turn the TV on while she's reading, and so he just stands there. Waiting. Watching.

Mom should be home any minute. She usually gets home around four fifteen, except on Mondays, when she gets home at five. M used to carry their house key in her backpack but she kept losing it, so Mom makes her wear it on a string around her neck. Under her clothes. M thinks it's embarrassing. And itchy. Ben just wishes he had his own key, because sometimes M misses the bus and has to walk home, and when his bus drops him off, she's still not there and he has to wait. It would be easier if they were closer in age. Then their grades would be in the same school and they wouldn't have to take separate buses. Only M would probably hate that. Because she would never want him trailing after her all day long. Not in front of her friends, anyway. Or so she says. Ben doesn't think she's made any, even though she claims she has. He hasn't met any of them, though. And M never likes anybody, so how could she have gone and made friends? Don't you have to like your friends?

"Can we go outside?" he asks as his sister turns the page. M's eyes flit across him suspiciously, the rest of her body perfectly still. He's always asking Mom to take him for walks, but he never expresses any interest in going out without her. A golden retriever. That's what M calls him. Loyal as a golden retriever.

"No," she replies decidedly, her attention returning to the novel.

"Why not?"

Releasing a short puff of air through her nose, M shifts her position on the couch so that she's facing her brother, hugging the book to her chest. "Do you *want* to get kidnapped?" They haven't gone over stranger danger in his class yet, but M did years ago. She's saying this to scare him.

"No," he manages meekly.

"Exactly."

"What about the backyard?"

It's fenced in, which is one of the things Mom liked about it in the first place. It's only a chain-link fence, but still. She's said a few times now that maybe one day they will get a dog. "But we already have our puppy" is M's standard reply. She likes to ruffle Ben's hair when she says this. It would annoy him, except it's the only time M ever acts like maybe she just might like him a little.

"If you want to go, then go," she grumbles. She opens the book and continues her reading. For a moment Ben hesitates, waiting to see if she will finish the chapter and get up to follow him. When she doesn't budge, he heads into the kitchen, and from the couch he hears M call after him, "Don't go near any unmarked vans!"

Ben still finds it strange that the back door is in the middle of the kitchen, right between the cabinets and the breakfast table. He thought this would be what garages were for, but here you get into the garage from the laundry room. Mom loves having a laundry room—maybe more than she even loves having a house or a backyard.

Ben twists the round golden lock above the handle and swings open the door. It isn't as heavy as the front door, which he's always forgetting. He nearly trips stumbling back from the force of it.

He falls against a chair, which then knocks the table, which regains M's attention. "And don't break yourself!" she adds sharply.

Mom would definitely tell him to wear a jacket, but Ben doesn't feel like going back to the front hall and facing his sister. He walks out onto the grass and pulls the sleeves of his sweatshirt over his hands. It's chilly out, but not as bad as it had been this morning when they left for school. Not too breezy. Not too crisp. Fresh.

He stops as he reaches the fence, propping his elbows up on it and leaning his chin against his arm. Their backyard doesn't face another house, it faces the curve of the street behind theirs. He wishes there was a house there, that way there would be people to watch—or at least hear—from the kitchen. He really can't get used to how quiet it is around here.

He closes his eyes and listens. Somewhere in the distance he hears a truck gurgling along and a bike bell ringing. He does like the grass, even if it is pretty much dead now. When they'd moved in it had been so green. So soft between his toes.

"You look like you're thinking," comes a voice from the darkness. Ben opens his eyes and looks left—the direction from which the voice had come—to see Mrs. Yeung in the backyard next door. She's holding a bag of seed for the bird feeder. M thinks it attracts more squirrels than birds, but Ben likes how the feeder brings out all the cutest critters.

"No," Ben replies, shaking his head. Mrs. Yeung never seems to notice that he gets quiet around adults. Instead, she smiles at him like she knows him, which almost makes him believe that she does.

"It's all right if you are. Thinking is good."

Mrs. Yeung says this as she opens the top of the feeder, which hangs on a branch of the yard's only tree. She pours some of the seeds from the bag into the tube. She then fastens the lid back on, and as she's making sure it is on tight, Anna Mae comes running out the Yeungs' sliding glass door—her dark, long hair whipping behind her. "Make sure there are lots of yellow ones!" she tells her mother. "Frederick likes the yellow ones."

Mrs. Yeung nods, even though most of the seeds in the feeder look brown, not yellow. Quickly Anna Mae notices Ben and, without waiting for him to ask, comes over and puts her arms on the fence between them. "Frederick is a bluebird," she explains. "My dad thinks he's flown south for the winter, but I saw him yesterday. He's always hungry."

Flashing both children a grin, Mrs. Yeung disappears back into the house, and Ben watches the way Anna Mae doesn't follow her. Instead, the girl stays at the fence. Feeling like he's supposed to do something, he goes to meet her at the side of the fence that separates their yards.

Anna Mae likes to talk, which is fine, since he likes to listen. When they'd first moved here, she told him that she was named after an actress called Anna Mae Wong. Ben didn't know who that was, but he'd nodded like he did. And this had made Anna Mae smile. They aren't in the same class at school, but they're the same age. Mom likes this—the idea of him having someone so near to get along with. And he does get along with Anna Mae, even if they still aren't exactly friends.

Anna Mae tilts her head. "Whatchya doing?"

He shrugs.

Her head stays at that odd angle as she studies his face, then it straightens abruptly and her eyebrows turn inward. "Have you ever kissed anybody?" she asks.

"No."

"Can I tell you a secret?"

"I don't know."

"Steve wants to kiss you."

Ben's brow bunches up confusedly.

"It's true," Anna Mae goes on. "He told Billie and she told me. It's a secret, though. So don't tell anyone."

Billie and Anna Mae are best friends, but he didn't know Billie was friends with Steve. Are boys allowed to be friends with girls? "Boys don't kiss boys," he tells her, trying to mimic M's way of sounding like she knows exactly what she's talking about when she's talking about it.

Anna Mae laughs. "Yes, they do. Kate's aunt is a girl and she lives with another girl, and Kate says they kiss all the time. It's the same thing."

"Why would Steve want to kiss me?"

"Maybe he likes you."

Ben doesn't particularly like the idea of kissing anybody. He's never even kissed M on the cheek, and she's his own sister. He kisses Mom on the cheek all the time, but that's different. Or at least he thinks it's different.

And as for liking him . . .

Why would anybody like him?

"You should only kiss someone if you love them," Ben tells her, because that's what Mom has always told him. Even though he's seen her kiss lots of people. And she couldn't possibly love them all.

Anna Mae shrugs. "I would kiss Steve if he wanted to kiss me."

Ben doesn't say anything.

"He has really nice hair," she adds, as if having been asked for a justification. Ben wonders suddenly if he has nice hair. He wants to ask, but doesn't. Anna Mae looks around his yard, which has a chipped patio table with no chairs and a crooked cement walkway that's only half finished. It was like this when they'd moved in. He wishes their yard was more like Anna Mae's. They at least have that beautiful tree.

The girl's curious gaze slowly crawls up the side of the house, resting somewhere on the second floor. "Is that your room?" she asks. Ben turns around to look where she's looking and realizes she's talking about the window with the sticker. One of the upstairs windows has a little fireman sticker, which Mom says is to let firemen know where the children are if there's ever a fire. She doesn't have a sticker, though, which worries Ben a lot. Especially at night. Firemen would need to find her too.

"No," he says. "That's my sister's. You can't see my room from the backyard. Just the front."

"Do you lock your window?"

"No."

"You should lock your window," Anna Mae tells him. "Otherwise, the cat burglar can climb up and get in."

"But it's upstairs," he says, as if it should be obvious. And it's true. They don't even have a fire escape like they used to—how could anything ever get all the way up there?

"A cat burglar can climb anything," she insists.

"What's a cat burger?"

"A cat *burglar*." She giggles. "Someone who breaks in at night and takes things." Anna Mae glances over her shoulder as if she might be caught and punished for saying this out loud. "My mom and dad don't think I know about him, but I heard them talking about it. They said he's gone into three houses already in Chase Hills and two in Parsippany."

A part of Ben wants to call her a liar, only Anna Mae has never sounded like a liar. Not even when she was talking about Steve and kissing and nice hair.

"Maybe he's the one moving your magnets," she suggests, only Ben doesn't think the Cat Man is doing that.

"No, that's the ghost."

"I told my mom, and she said there is no such thing as ghosts."

M has said exactly this to him. Mom too. But Ben doesn't believe them. Because if the ghost isn't moving things around the house, then who is? "Things never used to move before," he replies. "And now they move all the time. It's a ghost."

"Did someone die in your house?"

"I don't think so."

"If there's a ghost that means someone died," she tells him.

Ben considers this, quietly ashamed that he had not thought of it before. She's right. Does that mean someone died in their new house? Having a ghost is one thing, but the idea of someone having died there—this sends a chill up his spine to the very base of his skull. He shivers, but only a little, and hopes Anna Mae doesn't notice. "Maybe he's just lost."

"The ghost?"

He nods. "Maybe he got lost and just ended up here by accident."

"How do you know it's a he?"

This is another thing Ben has not considered. He'd just assumed the ghost is a boy, but maybe he's been wrong about that too.

"Ghosts can be girls," Anna Mae points out.

"Then maybe she is lost."

Anna Mae shrugs. "You should ask if the ghost has a name."

"Why?"

"Because everyone has a name," she says. "And maybe if you figure it out the ghost won't be lost anymore."

CHAPTER SEVENTEEN

AMY

FRIDAY, OCTOBER 15, 1993
10:30 P.M. (1 HOUR AND 30 MINUTES BEFORE MIDNIGHT)

Amy listens to the rhythm of the silence. Both children are asleep, or at least she hopes they are. She tucked Ben in herself and waited at the side of his bed until he'd finally drifted off. M had said she was going to bed, too, but Amy never obtained proof. She could go up and check now, but with the night they've had, she figures the kids can use the peace and quiet.

Amy flips the remote for the TV back and forth in her hands. She doesn't want to watch either movie anymore. Not after what happened with Mr. Mitchel. A part of her is even more than a little bit worried that he'll be back. Maybe she should call her mom, have her come and sit with her until Eleanor gets home. The only thing keeping her from making the call is the knowledge that she doesn't want to be seen like that—needing her mom to watch over her like she did when she was little.

Dropping the remote on the cushion beside her, she leans her head back on the couch and closes her eyes for one, two, five minutes. Maybe longer. When she opens them again everything about the room feels soft and fuzzy and familiar. She gazes up at the ceiling, and the longer she looks the more it feels like the lumps and imperfections in the paint are moving. Drifting.

There's a scene in *A Nightmare on Elm Street* where Freddy Krueger pushes through the wall above Nancy's bed, his body molding the wall around him. They used something stretchy for that. She doesn't remember what. Something with give, though. Wes Craven movies are creative like that.

A knock at the door sends a jolt through her bones, eviscerating whatever sense of calm she'd managed to compose. Leaping to her feet, she's desperate to get to the door before the kids hear it. Only the bat— where did she put the bat?

In the kitchen?

There is a second knock, softer this time, as Amy slides into the front hall and leans in to look through the side window. Her shoulders, tense and taut, ease when she realizes it is Miles, not Mr. Mitchel, who has returned.

Amy undoes the lock and opens the door. At the sight of her, Miles's expression quivers as if a part of him had been hoping she wouldn't let him in. "Hi," he says quietly, almost standoffishly. "Your folks said you weren't home yet, so I figured you must still be here."

Grinding her teeth, Amy doesn't say anything. He has that look on his face—one so worn and beaten it only could have come from having argued with his brother. She slides the door open a little further and, without a word, invites him inside. She locks the door behind him and the two stand idly in the hallway. Each waiting for the other to speak. To set the tone. Neither does, though. The awkwardness thickens. Taking up all the space around them. Thinning the air.

Growing more and more uncomfortable, Amy crosses her arms as if a chill has spread across the room. "What are you doing here, Miles?"

"You're right. My brother's a dick," he says. "I have to put up with it, but you don't. And it was unfair to bring them here without asking you."

Amy wonders if this is a conclusion he has come to on his own, or if his mother came to it for him. He tells the woman everything—or nearly everything—and Amy is pretty sure she is the reason his manners are generally better than those of other guys his age.

"These kids aren't ours to screw up, you know?"

"I'm sorry."

It's what he should have said hours ago, but the fact that he's saying it now, whatever the reason, softens Amy just a little bit. Unfolding her arms, she puts her hands out and slips them into his. They're freezing. And the warmth of her skin against his skin draws the teenagers closer together. "Are the kids in bed?" he asks.

Amy nods, her forehead pressed against his. "You can stay if you want. After all, you have my car."

He smiles, and it is a beautiful smile. Genuine. Warm. But suddenly, it falters. "I can't," he admits reluctantly. Amy's heart sinks. "My dad's been trying to fix the cable for like three hours. I told him I'd go back and help."

Amy almost laughs, squeezing his hands tight. His dad likes to believe he can fix everything. "That's okay."

"I can call him for a ride if you want your car back?"

Amy shakes her head. "Don't bother. I already called my mom. She's gonna come by later."

"You sure?"

"She sounded kind of happy about it. I think she misses driving me around everywhere, like when I was a kid. Those were the only times we ever really talked about anything important, you know?"

Miles doesn't, how could he? But he nods in such a way that makes Amy feel satisfied. Safe. "We're good? Right?" he asks. "You and me, I mean."

"Yeah. We're good."

They kiss, gently at first but then stronger—longer. She slips her tongue into his mouth, trying to keep Patrick and Sadie out of her head. Focusing on Miles—how good his hands feel going through her hair.

And the electricity coursing through her fingers as they slide across his shoulders. She focuses on his lips. His skin. How he smells like fall, like the wind outside. She wants him in a way that feels real—realer than it's ever felt before. It takes every millimeter of her focus to pull away, and she does pull away, because she made a promise to Eleanor. No sex. Even though her heart is beating and she can't breathe. It's not a panic attack—no, this is different, better. Similar to a panic attack but the opposite in every way that matters.

She waits for Miles to look disappointed, but he's too busy grinning. The electricity. He must feel it too. He can't stop smiling at her. It's such a goofy, adorable smile. "Want to come over tomorrow?" he asks. "My parents are going out."

"I'm watching the Baker kids."

"When do you have to be there?"

"Five."

"You can stop by before you go," he says. "If you want to, I mean."

She resists the urge to fix her hair. "Yeah. I'd like that."

"You would?"

She nods, leaning in again and pressing one more kiss against his lips. She wonders if she's blushing too, or if it's just him. "What time?"

"Is two okay?"

"Yeah."

He kisses her again and it's almost like she's forgotten how to breathe. "God, you're beautiful," he says, almost like he's bewildered by the fact that she's right there in front of him.

Her breath catches in her throat. They kiss again, this time with more tongue than is probably needed to get the job done. "You should go," she says as they part, a giggle at the back of her throat. "Last time your dad tried to fix something he nearly set the kitchen on fire."

Miles laughs. "That's how we learned the fire extinguisher was expired."

"Go," she urges, not because she wants to see him leave but because she's afraid of what she might do if he stays any longer.

"Tomorrow," he says.

She nods, ushering him to the door. "Tomorrow."

As sorry as she is to see him go, Amy isn't prepared for the hole his absence leaves until the door is closed and bolted behind him. She wants to rush to the window—to watch him get in the car—but knows that is the sort of thing silly girls do. And she'll be damned if she becomes silly just for him. Her hands are trembling. She can still taste his tongue in her mouth.

Returning to the living room, Amy pulls the *Halloween* tape out of the VCR and puts it back in the case. Then she goes to her backpack, still lying by the chair, and zips it inside. It's a shame she didn't get to watch the other movie. The Bakers are very strict people. No television at all—not for the kids and not even after they go to bed. The only reason they have a TV in their home is because Mr. Baker says Mrs. Baker likes *Jeopardy!*

Amy sits on the floor in front of the backpack and, in the privacy of the empty downstairs, fixes her hair. That's Miles's go-to when they make out, his fingers creating knots in her hair. It feels good—really good—but she can't look a mess when Eleanor gets back. Or when her mom picks her up.

Twisting around, she checks the time on the VCR. It is after eleven. Maybe Eleanor was wrong and this accountant is a good dancer. Last time Amy was over, Eleanor and her date went dancing after dinner. Apparently, the guy wasn't very interesting and talked too much—Eleanor hated him within the first ten minutes—but she's not one to turn down a night of dancing. No matter how boring her partner.

Fidgeting with her ring, Amy looks around the room. There are no toys to pick up with the Mazinski kids. They don't leave any out. Amy sees the bat next to the front door. She picks it up and brings it into the kitchen where she notices the pizza boxes are still sitting on the counter.

Amy puts down the bat and awkwardly lifts one of the boxes, trying to flatten it so she can fold it into fourths and shove it in the garbage. Only she isn't really holding it right, and the wax paper from within flutters onto the floor. Amy swears and puts the box down and lifts the paper, which has left a greasy, cheesy print across the kitchen floor. Amy goes to the sink, takes off her ring and puts it on the counter, and grabs some paper towels. She squirts a dime's worth of soap onto them before soaking them with water.

Kneeling, she presses the soapy water against the floor, trying especially hard to ensure that the oil has left no mark. Then she tosses the paper towels, pulpy and falling apart, into the other pizza box before retrieving another wet paper towel to rinse away the soap.

She's in the process of trying to dry the linoleum when she hears a marked thud from upstairs. Or maybe not a thud. Maybe just a creak from the pipes.

Careful not to drop anything, Amy brings the boxes over to the garbage and brushes in all the used paper towels and wax paper before flattening the boxes and folding them up tight and shoving them in too. Then she goes into the hallway and listens by the stairs, just to be certain what she had heard was not one of the kids getting up. Or falling out of bed. She used to do that when she was younger—kick around so much in her sleep that she'd wake up just in time to hit the floor. Or nearly hit the floor. Usually, the blankets were already there to break the fall, but still the impending impact sent a jolt through her. Each and every time.

Amy flips the switch for the light in the kitchen off. The less Eleanor has to do when she gets home, the better. Heading back into the living room, she drops onto the couch and stares up at the ceiling, noticing every subtle crease in the paint. The yellowness of the lamplight makes the blue look almost green. Fidgety, she pulls herself up to turn off the living-room light. When she returns to the couch, she drops into it. The light in the hallway is still on for when Eleanor gets back, but at least maybe Amy can just decompress until then. It's been a long night.

She hopes the date went well. For Eleanor's sake. She deserves a good time. Especially with the shit of an ex she has stalking around. At the very thought of him, Amy groans. It's her fault—maybe not the him-showing-up part, but she'd allowed him to get inside. To scare the kids. She thinks of what Mira had said about her brother. *He's safer scared.*

We're all safer if we're scared.

There's another creak, this time from the kitchen. Only it doesn't sound like the walls grumbling. It sounds like the back door.

Amy sits up, at first wondering if Eleanor just decided to come around to the other side of the house. Only there's no gate in the back-yard. Her feet slip onto the carpet and she listens. The distinctive *click* of a door closing echoes through the house impossible for her imagination to fabricate. She stands up rather quickly and crosses into the hallway, stopping at the mouth of the kitchen. It's dark but not too dark, and she can make out the shape of a figure there, facing the window, shoulders hunched forward as whoever it is bends over the counter.

A ghost. Ben's ghost. Every cell in Amy's body is screaming that it can't be. Ghosts aren't real. Only, she's seen that trope before. The Freelings don't expect their house to be haunted in *Poltergeist*, but it is; they have to come to terms with that. To make it through. To survive. Ghosts aren't real and they aren't real and they aren't real, until they are.

Amy doesn't speak. Doesn't move. Her eyes are beginning to burn because she's too afraid to blink. Her stomach has already made a break for it, trying to claw its way up her throat.

The figure must sense her presence—her fear—because it turns.

"Where are the peanuts?" it asks.

Only *it* is not an *it*. And Amy knows this story too.

It was late—later than her mother had said they'd be home, not that Amy was surprised. Her parents were always optimistic in their plannings, never taking into account the realities of traffic and parking and Uncle Andrew's tendency to say in fifty words what could have been conveyed in five.

Amy pulled herself up on the couch, draping her arms over the back to better watch Sadie in the kitchen. The babysitter was wiping crumbs off the counter with a towel. Their cookies sat proudly centered on the stove, arranged atop a novelty plate Amy's parents had gotten in Ocean City, the one with hand-painted seahorses decorating the rim. Amy yawned and Sadie let out a low chuckle. "You tuckered out, peanut?"

Amy shook her sleepy head.

"It's okay if you are."

When Charlie and Donnie were in charge, they never asked Amy if she was tired. They'd just argue about which one of them Danielle Deluca had a crush on and start another John Carpenter movie. Then again, she'd never had one of her anxiety episodes in front of Charlie and Donnie.

Quietly, Amy watched the way Sadie continued to tidy up the kitchen. The babysitter was methodical in her approach, working counterclockwise to make sure everything was in its right place. She'd done the same when they were putting all the jewelry and the hats away. They'd said nothing about the episode since it happened, but Amy preferred it that way. And it had been fun, trying on her mother's fancy rings. Amy wondered if she could ask her mother for that gold-and-silver ring when she was older. Her mom rarely ever wore it, and Amy had liked the texture—the certainty of its heaviness in her hand, as if it were helping to keep her tethered to the ground. Safe on her own two feet.

At some point Sadie caught Amy watching her, or maybe she'd been aware of it all along, and a grin crooked in the corner of the babysitter's mouth. "What?" she asked.

"I think the counters probably look better now than they did before you got here."

Sadie laughed. "Whatever you're going to do in life, do it well," she said. "There's no point in ever doing anything halfway. That's what I tell my sister all the time."

"Do you like that?"

"Like what?"

"Having a sister," said Amy.

Sadie gave her a sympathetic look and exhaled quietly. "Sometimes. And sometimes I wish I was an only child, like you."

"Being an only child is boring."

Sadie came around the counter, sat down on one of the stools, and folded her arms. "Most things in life are boring," she conceded. "It's up to you to make them less boring."

Amy was beginning to feel a little less shy. "How?"

"Well, that part's subjective," the babysitter said with a shrug. When Amy frowned and knit her brow, she continued. "Subjective means it's based on your own personal feelings. What you want to do, not what other people tell you to do."

Instead of comforting the child, this made her frown deepen.

"What? What is it?"

"I don't know what I like," admitted Amy shyly.

"That's all right. You'll just have to figure it out. No one should be expected to know what they like right away. You learn from experience. From trying things."

"What if"—Amy almost held her breath for fear of asking—"What if the anxiety won't let me?"

Sadie looked at her with those knowing teal eyes. They were tender but hard at the same time, with a sparkle that shone like armor. "Life is going to happen whether you're scared or not. So you might as well live it."

"Is that what you do?"

"Absolutely."

CHAPTER NINETEEN

AMY

Sadie smiles and even in the dark it's a pretty smile. All bright and airy and short-lived. The fleeting nature of it only emphasizes what is now so clearly gone. Almost like an echo. A frown quickly appears in place of it. Your car isn't out front."

Amy doesn't know what she's doing here, doesn't even know how she unlocked the door. She should ask, but these questions are not willing to manifest themselves in her mouth. Not while her stomach is still lodged in the back of her throat. And so she stares and stares and stares and then says: "Miles took it home."

Sadie shrugs. "Guess you two didn't make up then."

Amy feels caught, like she's up sneaking around after bedtime and Sadie is going to scold her. Only Sadie is the one sneaking here. Amy swallows hard. For a time, they just stand there sizing each other up, trying to determine exactly which way this whole thing is going to go. Then Sadie shifts her weight, revealing the steak knife on the counter. And the SH minus the exclamation point carved into Ms. Mazinski's baseball bat.

The stomach in Amy's throat expands. Choking her. A spark of panic jolts through her body. She looks around, convinced that they can't possibly be alone. Sadie laughs.

"Pat isn't here," she assures her. "He hasn't got the stomach for it. Maybe if a house is empty, but I prefer it at night. Fully stocked. It's more of a thrill."

Sadie's eyes grow large, swelling with fierceness at that last word. *Thrill.* The sh was never a warning, it was a set of initials. Sadie's initials. Sadie Holt. sh. A taunt.

Just like that, every moment Amy has ever spent with Sadie spins through her brain like film on a spool. Searching for strange behavior from back when Amy was a child. Only, there is no montage to be found—no series of increasingly suspicious moments that can account for this. No movie magic. Just a level of surrealness that makes her feel like the floor is slanting beneath her. That question blooms in Amy's head again. If Sadie were a character in a horror movie, who would she be? Amy still doesn't have an answer, but she's certain that it would be different now from what she would have thought before.

"You stole Mrs. Johnson's earrings?" she asks, finally managing to slide her feet three inches forward, two inches back.

Sadie smiles modestly.

"And the Harringtons' remote?"

"Everyone takes a souvenir when they go on vacation."

"Why'd you cut up that man's feet?"

Sadie rolls her eyes, gesturing absently with her hands. "Why does anyone do anything?"

Amy frowns.

"I sat for them a few times," Sadie relents with a sigh. "He used to pay up front so that when he and his wife came home two hours late, he could just *forget* to pay me for the extra time."

Amy's frown remains unchanged.

"Or not. Maybe I'm making this up, and I did all that just because I wanted to." Sadie shrugs again. "I really thought you'd gone home," she continues, as if her surprise is somehow a consolation. Amy notices the ring on Sadie's finger. Her ring. She reaches for her own hand, as if it might contradict what she's seeing, but the ring isn't there. She must have left it on the counter.

Sadie follows Amy's gaze to the little lump of metal around her forefinger. "Is this yours?"

"You shouldn't be here," Amy finally manages, but it feels inadequate. *Get the fuck out* would be more suitable. *Get the fuckity fuck fuck OUT.* Only she doesn't say any of this. Because Sadie is Sadie and it is still Amy's instinct to defer to her former babysitter's seniority.

Green eyes shift beneath blond bangs. "You are no fun anymore, are you—Oh, man, I used to love these," Sadie smirks, moving forward and sliding Ben's book catalogue around to get a better look at the front page. "Are they big readers? The peanuts? Quiet kids are always big readers, aren't they?" She pauses, considering the generalization. "Except for you. But you always were something of a curiosity, weren't you? Stubborn, sure, but skin like eggshells."

"Ms. Mazinski is going to be back soon," Amy warns her, trying to strike a chord. Only, Amy doesn't know how to play the person in front of her. She doesn't know how to play anyone. Mira was the one who'd gotten Mr. Mitchel to leave. Not her.

Sadie hardly looks worried. No. In fact, she looks excited. That word pulses through Amy's brain again. *Thrill.* Sadie pulls her fingers from the catalogue. "I suppose you'll want to tell Ms. Mazinski I stopped by?"

Amy fidgets with her index finger, pinching at the tender, unprotected skin where her ring had been.

"You can't do that," Sadie says with a mischievous pout, shaking her head in disapproval. As if Amy has just asked for ice cream before bed even though her parents had instructed Sadie not to give her any. Sadie leans against the kitchen island between them. "You know you haven't changed one bit. I tried to help when you were growing up, I did, but here you are still coloring inside the lines."

"Get the fuck out."

"I'm not Pat. A cute little *fuck* out of you won't impress me."

"Get the fuck out. Now."

"Why?"

"*Why?*"

"Yes," Sadie continues. "Why? Because it's uncomplicated? I'm not *supposed* to be here and so my being here is wrong? Adults shouldn't be trusting their kids to random teenagers late at night, but here *you* are. Good. Bad. Right. Wrong. It's all subjective."

"This is breaking and entering."

"What do you mean? The door was unlocked."

Amy's brow knits. Eleanor would not have left it unlocked—and at no point did Amy unlock it. Sadie must have done that earlier. Before Amy kicked them out.

"Wow, there's really nothing beneath the surface, is there?" says Sadie, walking around the counter. Closing the distance between them. "I mean, this whole choirgirl thing is the perfect facade, but those movies you like—you really don't see something there? Something thrilling?"

The way Sadie says the word *thrilling* makes Amy's stomach churn. This is fun for her. And the more uncomfortable Amy gets, the more fun Sadie seems to have with it. "They're just movies," Amy manages. "Michael Myers isn't *actually* stalking babysitters."

"Maybe you just watch those movies because you don't have the guts for real life." Sadie pauses, tilting her head ever so slightly. "Same reason you're a babysitter. So you can hide yourself away. Play cute little games and read cute little books and forget the whole world. Only, bad things always happen to the babysitter in your movies, don't they?"

Amy tries to press the rolling list of home invasion movies from her mind. But as Sadie tucks a strand of hair behind Amy's ear, her brain splits open and they come pouring out. *Torso*, *Night of the Living Dead*, technically, *and*, *and*, *and* . . .

"Oh, come on!" Sadie almost sounds impatient. "Haven't you ever done something just because you wanted to? No. Of course not. Instead, you sit around and watch movies you'd be scared shitless to step inside."

"There's nothing wrong with that."

Sadie makes a face of what—disappointment? Disgust? No, it's pity. Pity galvanized in Sadie's big, blue eyes. "I used to be a lot like you," Sadie admits, her voice softening. It's almost like a plea. "So worked up over everything all the time. You've got to kill that fear before it kills you."

"And how do I do that? By dating a deadbeat and breaking into houses?"

Sadie smirks. "You think Pat is the judgmental one, but he doesn't care what I do. I can be anyone I want around him." Sadie stops and chuckles. "You know, you really would look better with bangs."

"I don't need bangs."

"No, what you need is to break free of yourself, little miss Amy. You clearly want to."

Sadie looks down at Amy's hands, and it is only in this moment that Amy realizes she's flexing them—has been flexing them—in and out of tight fists. Just like Sadie had taught her all those years ago.

Amy steps away to put some distance between them, but Sadie grabs her wrist. "Careful," she warns. "You wouldn't want to wake the peanuts."

Sadie's fingers are long and thin and freezing, but just as strong as Amy remembers them being from the time she got too close to the stove while they were making popcorn the old-fashioned way, and Sadie had to pull her away to keep her sleeve from catching on fire. Not cruel but not kind. Firm. Amy grits her teeth and yanks herself loose.

The pipes in the walls groan then. Someone upstairs must be running the water. One of the kids. One of the kids is awake. Amy turns to Sadie with deeper desperation, convinced she can reach the girl who taught her how to bake chocolate chip cookies. The girl who wouldn't let her burn her hand on the stove. "Please," begs Amy. "Just go. We don't have to talk about it or mention it again. Take the bat with you—as a *souvenir*. I don't care. Just leave."

"Or what?" Sadie replies, a pointedness to that smooth, delicate tone. As if she's just ordered Amy to bed or to finish her homework. But Amy holds her ground, even as the air in her lungs fizzles. She's afraid to take a breath—certain that if she were to inhale at this exact moment her lungs would fissure. "Okay. You want me to leave?" Sadie grabs the knife off the counter, points it at Amy's face with sugary-sweet menace aglow on her cheeks. Amy winces, but then Sadie lowers the knife, flips the handle, and presses it into Amy's hands. "Make me."

Amy gazes down at the blade as if Sadie has just handed her a live grenade.

"Go on," Sadie encourages. "Make me."

"Wha—no!" The half words tumble out of Amy's mouth, ashen and pathetic. There's no more air left to try again in a stronger voice, and so she merely mouths the word *no* over and over, shaking her head.

Sadie puts on that pout—the one that's starting to make Amy's skin crawl. "Oh, Amy." A half grin, as curious as it is corrosive, slips across Sadie's face. She takes the knife from Amy's limp hands and examines the blade playfully. Silence crackles between them. "People will let anyone into their house when they look like us, won't they?" Sadie sighs, toying carelessly with the knife's handle. "I mean, you are *adorable*, but you can't take care of anyone."

As if to prove her point, Sadie presses the knife against Amy's shirt—like she might cut through it to the skin and the muscle and all the inside parts that could so easily spill onto the outside. Only, Sadie doesn't do it. She doesn't gut her. Instead, she draws the knife away and laughs.

Amy makes a dash around the counter, scrambling for the baseball bat. Sadie, close behind, grabs Amy's shoulder just as Amy's hand grips the handle. She swings around to free herself, but her fingers slip and the bat flies across the room with a loud bang.

The kids. The kids will hear them. This thought twists Amy's stomach in a knot, and as it does, there's a sound: small bare feet on the floor. They both turn to see Ben standing there on the other side of the island, frozen like a deer that has already realized there's no point in running. It's too late. The car is coming for him. Something small and plastic drops from his hands, but he doesn't bend down to pick it up.

"Hello there, peanut," Sadie says, as if the boy has just walked in on them in the middle of a pillow fight.

"Ben." Amy instructs him cautiously, realizing the absurdity of what he is seeing—the knife in Sadie's hand. The scene that has been set in his own kitchen. "Go back upstairs, okay? Go back upstairs and wait for me there."

The boy doesn't meet her eye. Doesn't obey. Instead, he can't take his eyes off the knife.

"Listen to your babysitter," Sadie instructs. Her interreference makes Amy bristle.

Shaken from his trance, Ben looks up at Sadie with his little doe eyes. "I called the police," he says in a small, thin voice that is trying to be strong. "They're on their way."

Amy recognizes the tone immediately. He's trying to sound like his sister. He thinks he can make this go away with the same words Mira used to make their father go away. She catches a glimpse of Sadie, who has suddenly gone very still. Amy looks at the boy, panicked. "That's not true." She turns to Sadie. "He's lying."

Ben stands firm. "No, I'm not."

Amy takes a step in his direction. "Ben, this isn't like before."

Sadie says nothing, her expression fixed on the little boy. She's trying to assess the damage done. Calculate the space between here and real trouble.

"You better be lying to me, peanut," Sadie warns, her eyes a little icy. There's a change in her. The playfulness is gone. The words have actual weight. Like it isn't a game anymore. Not that Amy ever considered it to be one in the first place.

"Please," Amy says to Sadie. "Just go home."

The word *home* draws Sadie's attention away from the boy, but only for a moment. A chasm breaks through her icy eyes. Amy realizes she's said the wrong thing. Meanwhile, Ben stands up so straight he might as well be perched on his tippy-toes. "If you're still here when they come," he warns, bringing Sadie's focus back to him, "they are going to *arrest you*."

The chasm deepens. "That wasn't a very good idea, peanut," Sadie tells him.

Ben frowns. "I'm not your peanut!"

"He doesn't know what he's saying," insists Amy.

Sadie gestures in Ben's direction with the knife, and Amy can't tell if it's on purpose, if Sadie even realizes that she's still holding it or not. "Listen, now—"

"I'm—I'm not scared of you!" he shouts with all his little might.

It doesn't matter that he's lying—so clearly lying. Sadie snaps. She lunges for the boy and Amy throws all her weight into grabbing Sadie's arms and yanking her away from him. She yells for Sadie to stop—that it's a misunderstanding—but Sadie quickly overpowers her.

The ice in Sadie's eyes is all broken up now—floating in deep pools of endless blue—and somehow it is even more frightening than when her eyes were smooth and hard and unchanging.

They are face-to-face when the struggle reaches a stalemate. So close Amy can feel Sadie's breath on her cheeks. Sadie's expression is dark and molten. Amy's never seen anything like it before—not in real life. The gravity of it all begins to sink in. Amy feels dizzy. Uncentered. Like she might pass out or puke.

Then, she glances down and catches a glimpse of Sadie's white-knuckled hand. The one holding the knife. That hand is trembling. The dizziness stalls. Amy knows this sensation, like the shadow that lingers from dirt on celluloid. Fear. "He didn't call the police," Amy assures her as steadily and quietly as she is able.

"You're lying!" Sadie seethes.

"Why would I do that?"

"Because you're a fucking coward!"

Amy watches the way Sadie's eyes move unpredictably. How her hand continues to shake. The knife shaking with it. "Stubborn with skin like eggshells," Amy repeats. "You weren't just talking about me."

Sadie screams in defiance—a blood-curdling sound like the pig squeal they use in all the slashers. It's almost loud enough and big enough and brutal enough to knock Amy over. In fact, it just about does. Until Amy spots Ben at the other end of the kitchen. The wide-eyed terror on his face keeps her propped upright.

With all her strength, Amy brings her forehead down hard against Sadie's face. It's more strenuous than it looks in the movies. Sadie is taller, and Amy's head isn't at quite the right angle. The pain that unravels across Amy's head is almost enough to make her drop to the ground. The move does the trick, though. Sadie stumbles backward.

Head throbbing, Amy swivels and kicks Sadie in the shin as hard as she can. Sadie grabs her by the shirt and throws her against the sink, holding the blade to Amy's gut, only an inch from her navel. Amy can practically see the adrenaline radiating off Sadie's skin.

She pushes Sadie off and tries to run, but Sadie is fast. The two of them stumble across the room, the knife glinting in the sparse light between them. Amy pulls around and shoves Sadie into the counter, twisting as they struggle over the knife, when suddenly she hears a sound like a ripping seam. Only thicker. Meatier. She steps back and sees the handle of the knife sticking out of Sadie's side.

But the blade . . .

That means the blade . . .

Sadie slumps onto the floor. Blood begins to pool on the linoleum, expanding smoothly across the surface. This is the point in the movie when Sadie would say something clever—one last dig before her eyes go dim. Only her eyes are already dim. Amy's legs, weak and shaking, nearly buckle. At first, she wants to call out Sadie's name, but she's too terrified. Because she knows Sadie won't answer. *She won't answer, she won't answer, she won't answer, no she won't—*

Amy's feet shuffle back—not out of any particular survivalist instinct but because the blood is spreading toward her and she wants to get away. In place of air, vomit rises in her chest. She rushes to the back bathroom and barely makes it to the toilet before puking into the bowl. She retches and retches—until there is nothing left in her stomach—then goes ahead and retches some more. Her stomach is churning, curling, *writhing*. She can't breathe. There's no room to breathe, not with the way her empty stomach is squeezing—forcing her to gag even harder.

When at last her body can take no more, she curls into herself, arms wrapped tight around her belly, and realizes she can't scream. Or cry. Or emit any sound at all. All of that seems to have fled her body with the pizza now curdled in the toilet bowl. She closes her eyes and sees red. So much red.

She sits there for what feels like hours. Or maybe minutes. Time has become a fractured thing. She thought it would look different somehow— not that she ever really thought about blood. But she didn't expect it to look like it does in the movies. So red and rich and dark. And the sound— the knife going into . . . where it did.

She heard somewhere that in the movies they shove a knife into a watermelon to make the stabbing sound. They got that right too. She'd always assumed that movies were off—movies were dramatized—and they *were*, but some of it was realistic enough. More than some of it.

Again, she lurches over the bowl, a tiny dribble of bile sloshing against the ceramic.

She tries to stand, but her knees buckle almost immediately. Forcing her to try again. And again. Until, finally, she manages to stay on her feet. Shaking, she shuffles out of the bathroom and back into the kitchen.

Ben is standing over Sadie's body. Staring. Fear bright and fragile in his small face. Amy almost retches again when she realizes he's pulled the knife out. It's hanging helplessly in his hand.

What—why did he pull the knife out? Why did he touch it? What good could come from that? He's still holding it . . . how was he strong enough to pull it out?

Her brain can't process it all. There are too many questions. Too many fragments. Too much wrongness.

"B—Ben," she manages, and the little boy's face turns sharply to her. As if he half expected the sound to be coming from the ghost. Or even the dead girl. "Ben," she murmurs.

The knife drops to the floor, clattering loudly. Ben rushes into Amy's arms. Both of them are shaking. And Amy knows she should get up and pick up the phone, but she can't. Because Ben's arms are too tightly locked around her neck. Like he can't let go—won't let go. Never, ever again.

Her knees feel wet. The blood—she's kneeling in the blood. *Oh God.*

"Come here," she urges, still whispering. Because Mira hasn't come down yet, which means she hasn't seen the body. "Come here." She takes Ben by the hand and leads him into the bathroom. She closes the door behind them, red finger marks all over the eggshell-colored wood. "It's okay," she assures him. Or herself. Or the both of them. "It's all right. It's going to be all right."

Ben doesn't speak. Doesn't move. His toes are stained red with blood. The cuffs of his pajama pants too. It takes everything in Amy not to start dry heaving.

"Are you okay?" she asks, checking his arms. His chest. His face. As if whoever killed Sadie might also have harmed him—as if *she* wasn't the one who . . . who . . . who . . .

"You're gonna be okay," she says, trying to smile. Only in doing so she realizes she's begun crying. *Shit.* She wipes the tears from her cheek. Pennies. Her hands smell like pennies. Of course . . . from the blood . . . she's covered in it now.

"That was your friend," manages Ben at last, almost quizzically. This time Amy doesn't argue—doesn't say she and Sadie aren't friends. Weren't friends. Weren't.

Weren't. *Weren't.*

What a bulky word.

Amy's head nods up and down and up and down. It feels like her skull is just about ready to fall off and roll into her lap. "She . . . she was trying—she *did*—break in."

"Like the Cat Man?" he asks. He might as well be little Tommy Doyle asking Laurie Strode about the boogeyman in *Halloween*. Ben stares at her expectantly. Only she doesn't know what to tell him.

"I need to call the police," she tells him, whispering. Why is she whispering? She doesn't know. "I want you to wait in here. Understand? I want you to wait here and not come out until I say. Can you do that?"

Ben nods.

"Good boy. Stay here."

Standing this time is almost harder than it was before, but she forces herself to do it. She slips out of the bathroom and closes the door behind her. The moment she is out of Ben's sight her back falls against the wall, because Sadie's body is still there. Had she really thought it would move? That Sadie would just hop up and walk away? Barbara's brother's voice from *Night of the Living Dead* pulses in her ears. Is Sadie coming to get her?

No.

No, no, no, no . . .

Amy reaches for the phone and pulls it off the hook and starts to cry again, sobbing this time. Uncontrollably. Shaking so violently the phone tumbles out of her hand and she crumples onto the floor.

"Amy?" she hears from inside the bathroom.

"It's okay, Ben," she says. "Don't worry. It's going to be okay."

Only it isn't. And she knows it isn't.

And there is nothing she can do about it.

Was it even self-defense? Yes . . . of course . . . right? Right?

"Amy?" the boy calls again.

She tries to croak out a response, but the words are all jumbled in her mouth. Her stomach is twisted all the way up. She puts a hand to her mouth, partly to stifle the whimpering but also to see if she's actually breathing. Because she can't tell anymore. Her brain is sending all the wrong signals, crossing all the wrong wires.

The knob to the bathroom door turns and Amy jumps, nearly falling onto the floor. Ben steps out and she wipes the tears from her eyes. "Hey." The word comes out not as a word, but as a breath—her first real breath in at least a minute. She waits for him to go back into the bathroom, but he doesn't. Worried he'll see the body again, Amy waves him closer with her hand. Politely, as if she's just asked him to brush his teeth, the boy obliges. "You're safe, okay?" she says, taking his hands in hers. "Look at me. You're safe. No one is going to hurt you."

"Was she?" he asks. *She* meaning Sadie. The thief. The boogeyman. The dead babysitter. Only she hadn't been anyone's babysitter in a long time. And now . . .

Amy wants to say yes—not for him, but for herself. "I don't know," she admits. It's the truth. She has no idea what Sadie was going to do. Because Sadie had just as much fear built up inside her as Amy did—maybe more. Amy doesn't know what Sadie would or wouldn't have done to stay in control. The control she supposedly didn't believe in. And now Amy will have to live with that—live with the not knowing one way or another.

Ben wraps his arms around her, his chin pressed into the groove of her shoulder.

In this moment Amy tells herself that it was self-defense, that otherwise it would have ended with her on the floor with the knife and the blood and Ben standing over her. She had to do what she did.

She had to do it.

She had to do it.

The sound of the back door creaking sends a jolt through Amy's spine, all the way up through her neck, pushing a cascade of pins and needles rippling across her skin. She turns just as Tess is stopping by the counter, staring at Sadie's body on the floor.

Of course. Tess. Because Sadie didn't drive. Did they still have Miles's car?

Amy shifts protectively in front of Ben. A quiet rage bubbles beneath Tess's pale skin. "Go," Amy murmurs to the boy, pushing him toward the bathroom door. Tess looks up at them, her eyes as quiet and bright as dead stars. *"Go!"* shouts Amy, and Ben runs back to the bathroom, the babysitter close behind him. The boy stumbles into the room, and Amy, knowing there isn't enough time, pulls the door shut behind him, turning and bracing herself against the door as Tess lunges for her.

"What did you do?" Tess shouts, pinning Amy's neck. Amy can't breathe. Her arm falls as she fumbles for the door handle, desperate to hold it closed. So Ben won't try to open it and let her in. Because he'd be letting Tess in too. "What did you do?" Tess hisses again, hot air sticky in Amy's face.

Only Amy can't answer. Because Tess's fingers are still wrapped around her neck. Squeezing. Pressing into the flesh. She thinks of Bob— Bob and his body tacked onto the wall. Michael's head tilt. Only Tess isn't the killer here. Amy is the one who . . .

She doesn't recognize the crushing effect of Tess's grip—not until the air is sputtering low in her throat. She can't breathe—like that second before you throw up, when your throat is too full of bile to do anything other than retch. And Amy can't even do that. Her feet scrabble in the blood on the floor, slipping and sliding. Her grip on the handle loosens.

This isn't sustainable; Amy knows she can't keep this up. Everything in her body begins to feel light and loose and foggy. She can barely see straight. She closes her eyes, and the pressure on her neck—thick and heavy and absolute—vanishes in an instant. Air comes pouring into her lungs and she collapses onto the floor. When she looks up, she sees Mira standing in the kitchen, the baseball bat clasped in her hands. The bat still pointed out post-swing as she stares wide-eyed and shaking at the crumpled pile of Tess on the floor.

Tess doesn't stay down long, though. She rallies and scrambles quickly, pulling one of Mira's feet out from under her. The girl falls before she can scream. Tess moves to wrestle the bat from her, but before she can get it Amy crawls up, grabbing the bat from Mira as she stumbles back to her feet. Tess shouts one obscenity then another, all the while clawing at Mira. Amy takes a swing and can hear the bat crack against the side of Tess's head. The girl falls again. And this time she does not get up.

Mira shoots up, frantic, and Amy drops the bat. The sound of it hitting the floor makes both her and Mira jump. Amy looks from Tess to Sadie to the bathroom door. "Ben!" she calls. "Ben! Come on out now! Hurry!"

Immediately the handle twists. The door slips open. Ben lingers near the threshold—startled by the fact that there are now two girls on the floor when before there had been one.

Amy extends a hand. "Come on!" she urges. "Quick! Let's go!"

The boy tiptoes around Tess, keeping as close to the wall and as far from Sadie as he can. He navigates the linoleum the way a soldier might land mines. When he's close enough, Amy grabs him by the arm and guides him away from the blood on the floor. Quickly, she goes around Tess's limp body and, taking the girl by the arms, drags her into the bathroom. Amy has carried kids around before, but never someone her own size. It's difficult, and more than once she loses her grip and has to grab Tess's wrists again.

When she's finally got her in the bathroom, Amy runs out and closes the door. Only, if Tess wakes up again, she knows it won't hold, and so she grabs a chair from the table in the corner of the kitchen and drags it across the floor through the blood and to the door. She jams the back under the handle.

"Come on," Amy says to the children, taking both of their arms.

She pulls them into the front hall, but when Ben goes to leap onto the stairs, she catches him by the arm and pushes him into the living room.

The Fog. Elm Street. No good can come from running upstairs. If nothing else, movies have taught her that. She sits them down on the couch, peripherally conscious that Ben's bare feet are now tracking blood across the carpet.

"Wait! Phone!" Amy spits, trying to form a sentence. "Stay here," Amy instructs. "I need your phone! *Stay.*"

Ben's hand is still clasped tightly over Amy's. He doesn't seem capable of letting her go, but gently his sister pries his fingers loose and cups her hands over his.

Amy opens her mouth again, but no words come out. And so she runs back into the kitchen, trying not to look at Sadie's body. Trying, but . . . but . . . but . . .

She pulls the phone off the hook and gazes emptily at it. The receiver hums expectantly. Realizing she has to dial, the babysitter follows the cord to the cradle and punches in the numbers.

"Nine-one-one, what is your emergency?"

"There's been a break-in," Amy manages, her voice trembling. "One of the intruders is . . . dead. Fifteen Beacon Street."

The operator continues calmly, like she hears this sort of thing all the time. Does she? This is Chase Hills, after all. This isn't normal. Amy knows this isn't normal.

The operator asks for the address again and where Amy is now. She asks if she is safe, and Amy nods dumbly, muttering an audible reply only after some gentle prodding. "I have two kids with me," Amy adds, almost as if it's an afterthought. "They live here. I'm just the babysitter."

With that last word Amy thinks of Sadie and a shiver ripples down her spine.

The operator asks if there is a neighbor they can go to while they wait for help to arrive. Amy remembers Mr. Darren across the street and tells the operator that there is. The operator instructs her to go knock on Mr. Darren's door and wait there with the children.

After she hangs up, Amy goes to the fridge, trying but failing to ignore the body, the blood—and grabs the name and phone number of the restaurant. She shoves the piece of paper into her pocket. She'll call when they get to Mr. Darren's, though she doesn't know if Eleanor will still be there. Maybe they'd gone dancing after all.

When Amy returns from the kitchen, both of the kids are standing in the front hall again. Ben's squeezing his hands into fists and then loosening them, squeezing, then loosening. Mira comes and slips her hand into Amy's. The babysitter holds it tight. Then, Ben comes and tilts his blood-stained face upward. "Did the ghost make her do it?" he asks.

"What?" Amy asks, only having half heard him.

"The ghost," he says again. "Did it make her do bad things?"

Amy's gaze shifts to meets Mira's, but neither says a word. Mira eventually averts her eyes, and, at last, Amy shakes her head. "No," she tells Ben. "No, the ghost—it didn't make her do anything. Come on, we're going across the street."

CHAPTER TWENTY

BEN

FRIDAY, OCTOBER 15, 1993

6:08 A.M. (17 HOURS AND 52 MINUTES BEFORE MIDNIGHT)

Mom spins around from the refrigerator, hurrying across the room to slide the milk across the kitchen table. "Come on," she urges. "I want you both to eat before I have to leave."

M takes the milk, popping the cap off and pouring too much into her cereal bowl. Then she pours Ben's milk for him, because last time he tried it by himself he spilled it all over, and Mom was late to work.

"Hey," says Mom, eyeing M's bowl suspiciously as she sets Ben's dinosaur lunch box on the counter island beside M's paper bag. M absolutely refuses to carry a lunch box anymore. Says they are for babies. And when Mom tried to send her to school with old plastic grocery bags, M stopped eating lunch. Mom was not happy about having to buy the paper ones.

Mom nods at M's cereal bowl. "Half and half, remember?"

She means half Cheerios and half Lucky Charms, because, according to Mom, straight sugar will send them through the roof. Not that they have real Cheerios and Lucky Charms, but that's what they call them anyway. Their Cheerios are really Toasted O's and the Lucky Charms have some long name he can't remember. Mom buys these instead because they are cheaper and "exactly the same," only Ben knows that last part isn't true. Because "exactly the same" is grown-up for slightly but importantly different.

"Forty-sixty on Fridays," M reminds her. And she looks very pleased with herself about this. It was M, after all, who had bargained for them to have more Lucky Charms on Fridays. Ben appreciated this too. Because he doesn't really like Cheerios and he loves Lucky Charms.

"Yeah, forty-sixty, not twenty-eighty," Mom replies with a roll of her eyes. Only she doesn't make M pour out her bowl, and so his sister takes a spoonful and scoops it into her mouth and starts chewing happily.

"M, we're out of jelly, so peanut butter for the both of you," she says, dropping a little lump of tinfoil in M's bag, then Ben's box. M grumbles. "And sorry, B. We're out of Dunkaroos too." He frowns. They only get a box of Dunkaroos once a month, and now he'll have to wait until November to get more. "Fruit by the Foot?" she asks "Or those weird cookies that look like Santa Claus?

"Fruit by the Foot."

Retrieving a box from the cabinet, Mom pulls out a little package and tosses it into his lunch box like a basketball, scoring two or four or however many points a person scores when they get the ball in the basket.

When she's done, she zips up Ben's lunch box and grabs a bagel from the bag in the closet. "Amy is coming tonight," Mom reminds them, tearing off a piece of bagel and popping it into her mouth while she waits for the coffee to finish. Mom isn't very good at eating breakfast. Has never actually had a whole one for as long as Ben can remember. Only pieces here. Bites there. The reason she bothers at all is because she wants to set a good example, and because one time M tried to argue that she didn't want breakfast and shouldn't have to eat it because Mom didn't eat it either.

M groans, marshmallow mush on her tongue. "Why?"

"I told you," says Mom, coming and putting the cap back on the milk because M hasn't bothered. She returns the milk to the fridge and then stands there, bagelless hand on her hip. "I'm going out."

"Can't Aunt Patty do it? Or Aunt Layla?"

Both Layla and Patty are aunts who aren't aunts. They are Mom's friends from high school—her oldest friends. And they always used to hang around the apartment on the weekends. M likes them because they tell stories about Mom from when she was a kid, but they drink too much and smoke too much and laugh too loud for Ben. And they're always teasing him, which is probably why M likes them most. He frowns, and Mom, noticing that frown, comes and stands over them.

"Do you want Amy to watch you tonight?" she asks, directing the question at Ben and Ben alone.

The little boy nods.

"That's because he's in love with her!" grumbles M.

Ben shoots her a wounded look. "Am not!"

"Yes, you are—"

"Listen—listen—listen!" Mom's hands fly up between them. "Patty and Layla have their own lives. And Amy is really very sweet. She even charges us less than she charges other parents—because she likes us."

M leans back in her seat, sulking. Mom looks down at them with knowing eyes. "You'll have a good time with Amy, I promise."

M stirs her spoon aimlessly around in the bowl, unconvinced. Ben watches Mom watch them, a smile warming on her face. "It will be great," she assures them. "Just you wait and see."

Mom leans over and tucks M's hair behind her ear. M doesn't bristle. She just lets her do it. She'll fight with him all day and all night, but doesn't like to fight with Mom about anything. Not for long, at least.

Mom turns around and, finishing the last bit of her bagel, returns to the coffeepot and takes out a mug. "Oh, B! I found Nana's mezuzah," she says, pouring the coffee. She drinks it without any milk or sugar like most grown-ups because she says she likes the buzz. "It was wrapped in one of the towels in the closet. I don't know why, must have packed it that way so it wouldn't break."

Putting the pot back, Mom spins dramatically and folds her arms across her chest. Her hip falls casually against the edge of the counter. Her eyes narrow triumphantly. "Hung it up last night."

Ben drops his spoon, which clacks against the bowl and sends a little jolt of milk onto the table. Abandoning his chair, he runs into the front hall and stands on his tippy-toes to get a better look at the doorway. A little slip of silver glints in the early-morning light. Mom comes in after him and scoops the boy up into her arms so that he can get a better look.

"Just like yours," she says, fingering the mezuzah pendant around his neck. Ben doesn't move or speak. He only stares. The mezuzah is bigger than he remembered, or at least bigger than his own. The size of a crayon, only thicker. With curved edges and a small city engraved across the surface. He can't see it now, but he knows there's a scroll inside. Just like in his. Mom had shown it to him when she took it from Nana's house. Before they sold the place.

He runs a finger across the surface, brow bending at the funny angle Mom has put it at. It's crooked.

She giggles. "It's supposed to be like that," she assures him. "And it's going to protect us. Can you feel it?"

Ben nods, even though he doesn't feel anything, because he can tell Mom does. And Mom is usually right about these kinds of things. She can't read minds or tell the future, but she has a way of knowing what she needs to know when she needs to know it. This has always made Ben feel safe. Proud. Because Mom is better than other moms. She always has been.

"Nana had this for many, many years," she explains. "And it always kept her safe. That's why she lived to be so old."

Ben draws his finger across the nails holding the mezuzah in place—first the one at the top, then the one at the bottom. "Is it magic?" he asks.

Mom brushes a few stray hairs away from his eyes, smoothing them out carefully. "What do you think, B?"

He shrugs an I-don't-know shrug.

"I think it's probably a kind of magic," she tells him. "We had one when I was growing up."

"Did it keep you safe?"

"Yeah, it did. And it brought me good luck too. I met your dad, didn't I?"

Ben frowns.

"Don't, B. Listen—he's the reason I have you. And your sister. And being with the two of you is the safest place in the big, whole wide world. Did you know that?"

He nods.

"You did?" She laughs, pretending to be surprised. "How? You must be a mind reader."

"You say it all the time."

"Doesn't mean it's not true," Mom tells him. She touches the mezuzah on the wall with her free hand, the tips of her fingers lingering against the metal. "Do you like it?"

He nods again. He likes that they finally have a real one—and a real door to put it at. A real home. And Mom must be right, he decides. It will protect them. Watch over them.

Only good things will happen here.

Because this is their new life.

And because Mom never lies.

CHAPTER TWENTY-ONE

AMY

SATURDAY, OCTOBER 16, 1993
1:04 A.M. (1 HOUR AND 4 MINUTES AFTER MIDNIGHT)

If Amy half closes her eyes, the flashing red lights atop the police cars swirl in a sea of color. She's tired but in that too-tired way that makes it impossible to calm down. The blood in her veins is thrumming, as if to reaffirm that it continues to flow as it should. That's it's inside her body instead of out.

Besides, every time her brain goes quiet for even a second, she sees Sadie lying on the floor in the Mazinski kitchen. And when this happens the flashing police lights turn to swirls of blood before her eyes.

Ben's face is pressed against her arm, his arms covered by a blanket one of the officers had draped over him. It's already slipping off his shoulder, and Amy is afraid to fix it for fear of disturbing him. She can hear the quiet rhythm of his breathing—deep, steady breaths—and is grateful that he isn't awake to see the neighbors peeking between window curtains and standing out on their front lawns to shake their heads in dismay.

Mira is quiet on Ben's other side, her hands folded across her knees. She is very much awake. On high alert. But still. She hasn't taken her eyes away from the house—not since they were sat down on

Mr. Darren's stoop and told to wait. Mr. Darren is inside making them tea. Amy hates tea, but she didn't have it in her to object. From the moment they showed up at Mr. Darren's door all bloody—the children bleary-eyed and bewildered—he's been fussing. At least for now, preparing tea seems to be the best he can do to feel useful. Amy is grateful for his kindness. He wanted to call Amy's parents while they were waiting for the police to arrive, but Amy begged him not to do it. Not yet. She was ashamed. Scared. Terrified of what her father would say or her mother would think. The pair of them probably fell asleep in front of the television waiting for her call home for a ride. She wonders what will happen when they wake up in the middle of the night and realize that she isn't there—that she hasn't so much as left a message on the machine. She will have to let Mr. Darren contact them soon.

As they sit underneath the porch light on the steps, Mira retrieves something from the pocket of her jeans. It's a little dinosaur figurine made out of hard plastic. She reaches for her sleeping brother's hand, slips the toy into his palm, and folds his fingers around it. Then she sits back up straight. Returns her attention to the house across the street. Her house. The one wrapped up in police tape like a macabre gift box.

The police found Miles's car parked around the back of the house. Patrick must have let Tess and Sadie take it. Or maybe Sadie just stole the keys from him. As soon as the first ambulance arrived, Tess was taken off to St. Mary's Memorial Hospital. Amy is wondering when they'll bring Sadie out, hoping Ben won't wake up to see a zipped-up bag on a gurney being rolled across his front lawn.

Suddenly, a pair of headlights pour stark white light down the street. Amy and Mira turn their heads in unison to see the car approaching. It comes to stop just behind the police barricade, and Eleanor jumps out, her green dress a shimmering jewel in the night. Amy's heart tries to claw its way up her throat. It's all her fault. She promised to look after Ms. Mazinski's children and instead she let in and then proceeded to stab a burglar. She's useless as a babysitter. As a person. Sadie was right. She can't take care of anyone, let alone herself. She's no Nancy Thompson. No Laurie Strode. She's more like Angela in *Night of the Demons*, thinking it's a good idea to hold a séance in a goddamn funeral parlor. The one who is, literally, unleashing hell upon everyone around her.

Eleanor and the officer exchange words—terse ones based on the way Eleanor is gesticulating. At last, Eleanor throws up her hands and shouts what Amy is pretty sure to be "Fuck off!" at the cop before pushing past him and heading straight for Amy and the children on Mr. Darren's stoop. As she gets closer, Amy sees that her face is very pale, with eyeliner smudged below her eyes. Has she been crying? Amy can't tell. She doesn't know what transpired when the police finally managed to get ahold of Ms. Mazinski. How much they told her.

The Japanese restaurant was closed when they tried the number Eleanor had left on the fridge, but Mira was able to offer up a list of places with live bands and dancing that her mother frequented. They went through the phone book and called each one until they found her.

As if sensing his mother's nearness, Ben stirs groggily. As soon as his eyes focus on her, however, he leaps to his feet and throws himself into Eleanor's arms. Mira remains seated. Pensive. Amy recognizes the framework of guilt in Mira's hunched, brittle posture. Like Amy, Mira is disappointed in herself for having allowed the evening to reach this point. Only, it hadn't been Mira's responsibility to prevent any of this from happening. She is the child. Amy, the adult.

"B," Eleanor says to the top of Ben's head as he hugs her. "My B, my B, my B."

He looks up into her face eagerly. "It protected us!"

"What's that?" says Eleanor. Her voice is calm but Amy can tell it's forced, with hard edges and strained vowels. She was definitely crying in the car. Amy's stomach twists. What it must take to make Eleanor Mazinski cry.

Ben holds up his mezuzah pendant for his mother to see. "This one protected me and the one on the front door protected M and Amy!"

Mira rolls her eyes and for a second—one fleeting, faltering second—things almost feel normal. Amy stands up as Eleanor murmurs gentle words of reassurance in Ben's ear. The mother kisses the top of her boy's head not one or two but three times before holding him close to her body and looking up at Mira. "Come here," she mouths over Ben's head, and the girl rises to her feet. Eleanor welcomes Mira into her outstretched arm, pulls the girl close and kisses her. For once, Mira doesn't bristle at the attention. Instead, she gazes up at her mother with the calm, careful eyes of a girl who has spent too much of her life worrying about other people. Eleanor looks at Amy. "They said it's not Dan."

Amy shakes her head. "No—he was here, but he left hours ago."

"Amy kicked him out," Mira adds suddenly.

Ben nods. "With the baseball bat."

Eleanor's eyes widen, and Amy wants to shake her head, explain that it was really Mira who got rid of Mr. Mitchel, and that she was only responsible for bringing Sadie into their home.

"I'm—I'm sor—" Amy can barely speak. Her voice is hoarse, aching from having held back the urge to sob for so long. But she has to say it. She has to say it because she means it. More than anything, she means it. "I'm—I—I—"

Eleanor frowns. "Amy."

"I didn't mean to—I should—I should have—"

Panic. Amy can feel it. Rising in her chest. Swelling against her ribs until she feels like they might splinter. Her vision is about to tunnel, she's sure of it, when suddenly Eleanor places a hand on her forearm. The shock of it is enough to startle Amy, if not stave off the panic entirely.

It looks as if Eleanor's own expression might split into one of pain, but she holds fast. "You are my guardian angel," she declares with more tenderness than Amy knows herself to deserve.

"But it's all my—"

"You protected my kids."

"No, but—"

"You protected *my kids*," Eleanor repeats, no room in her cadence for negotiation.

Maybe the police didn't explain properly. Maybe there hadn't been time on the phone. "Sadie Holt"—saying the name aloud now makes Amy's insides scream—"She got in because of me. She chose your house because of me."

Eleanor squeezes her forearm gently. "That's not your fault."

"It is . . ." Amy stammers. She can't stop herself. Hot tears streak down her cheeks. "Don't you understand? It is all my fault. I have been the most irresponsible, careless—"

Eleanor stops her. "We don't always get to decide where we'll be when life goes to shit. Believe me. But my kids had you," she continues. "They had you to watch over them. Any mother in this world should be so lucky."

Amy's lips part. It's absurd. Obscene. She feels like Sally riding away bloody and screaming and laughing at the end of *The Texas Chainsaw Massacre*. Or Laurie exhausted and crying into her hands at the end of *Halloween*. Only, she's not laughing. Not curling up into a ball. There are no closing credits. No sequels. Because she's not a movie heroine. She's flesh and blood and bone. And when the sun comes up, she'll still feel like hell.

We're safer when we're scared. That's what Mira had said earlier. But was it true? Sadie said to kill the fear, but then she was so unprepared to lose control that it cannibalized her, unleashed something ugly. Something cruel.

Still holding tight to his mother, Ben reaches out with one arm and takes Amy's hand, dried now with flaking blood, in his own. She looks down at him. He's so small. She hadn't noticed before—the enormity of his smallness. Perhaps because she'd felt small too. As helpless and vulnerable as the children she watches. Amy squeezes his hand and he squeezes back, ever so slightly, pulling her closer.

A chill sharpens in the air. Amy thinks of her grandfather's coat hanging on the banister at the Mazinski house. Her decoy skin. But there's nothing left to hide.

The police lights dotting the street continue to swirl. Soon, Mr. Darren comes outside and, with only the briefest glance at the chaos that has engulfed Beacon Street, tells them all that the tea is ready.

ACKNOWLEDGMENTS

I never thought this would be *the* book. It took me five years to get this story right. It was not the novel through which I met my agent. It wasn't even the second manuscript I showed her. But it's the one. I've been writing novels since age eight and this is the one that resonated with all the right people at all the right moments to result in the finished book you now hold in your hands. It's been an incredible journey, and I owe a great many people for this opportunity.

Everyone says their agent is incredible but my agent *is* incredible. I signed with Jennifer Weltz at the Jean V. Naggar Literary Agency in 2015, two years before I even started work on *Midnight on Beacon Street*. Over the years she has been a pillar, believing in my work even when I feared I was wasting her time. She is an exceptional agent, astute editor, and all-around wonderful person. I can never thank Jennifer, Ariana Phillips, Cole Hildebrand, and everyone at the Jean V. Naggar Literary Agency enough.

I owe a great deal to David Howe, my editor at Harper Perennial. His enthusiasm for this project is incredible. I gave him a non-linear 1990s babysitter book boiling over with horror movie references and he has championed it in a way I never thought possible. Thanks to Suzy Lam for being a wonderful production editor and Jane Cavolina for being an amazing copy editor. Thank you to Joanne O'Neill for the cover design and Jen Overstreet for the interior design.

I want to thank my early readers, who gave me their time and inspired me with their insight. J. A. W. McCarthy, Patrick Barb, Aiden Merchant, Cay Leytham, and Matthew Brandenburg all offered valuable feedback and encouragement during the revision process. They are each remarkable writers in their own right as well, and you should seek out their work. I'd also like to thank writers Jaye Viner, Grace R. Reynolds, Christie Donato, and Danielle Robertson for their continued support and friendship.

Special thanks must be given to Elizabeth Anne Schwartz—a longtime friend and incredible writer who beta read many of my *Beacon Street* revisions and who put up with me emailing her title after title idea until I finally found the right one. I am better for your friendship and the world is better for your talent.

This book could not have been written if not for my family. My brother and sister were the cool teenagers I looked up to growing up. They are the reason I have such a soft spot for the '90s. Shout out to Kathleen, with whom I rented *Scream* and *Final Destination* from the local video store in 2003—cementing a love of horror that *Are You Afraid of the Dark?* had kindled back in elementary school. Thank you to my nieces and nephew, without whom I wouldn't have known the first thing about looking after children. I first began writing *Midnight on Beacon Street* when I was babysitting my two youngest nieces three times a week. If Mira and Ben resonate as authentic children, it is because of these four amazing humans who have taught me so much about being a good aunt.

I need to shout from the rooftops how much my mom and dad have done for me as a person and as a writer. At six years old I told them I wanted to be a novelist, and not once did they ever question my ability to become one.

Mom (known as Pauline Verona to those who aren't her children), you have read everything I've ever written. I know you prefer mysteries to horror, but that has never hindered your enthusiasm for my work. You are my biggest champion and my best friend. All the best parts of me were instilled by you. Thank you for raising me, loving me, and believing in me as a storyteller. No matter how much I celebrate your support, it will never be enough. I am who I am because of you.

Last but not least, thank you to my little dog. Phoebe, you don't read, but you have watched patiently for the past ten years as I've written and rewritten each word. I'm so glad we belong to each other. My world is a better place because of it.

Emily Ruth Verona received her bachelor of arts in creative writing and cinema studies from the State University of New York at Purchase. In 2014 she won the Pinch Literary Award in Fiction. She is a Bram Stoker Award nominee, a Jane Austen Short Story Award finalist, and a Luke Bitmead Bursary finalist. Her publication credits include fiction and poetry featured in several anthologies as well as magazines such as *The Pinch*, *LampLight*, *Mystery Tribune*, *The Ghastling*, and *Nightmare Magazine*. Her essays and articles have appeared online for Tor.com, *BookBub*, *Litro*, *Bust*, and *Bloody Women*. In 2023, she founded the horror book blog *Frightful*. She lives in New Jersey with a very small dog.